INHERITING EVIL

INHERITING EVIL

K S Logan

CHAPTER ONE

"PURSE. *NOW.*"

"Okay, okay. It's in the front," Grace said. He led her to the storefront, keeping her neck crooked tightly in one arm.

"Hurry up, bitch," he growled in her ear.

She grabbed her purse from behind the counter and handed it to him. He let go of her and rummaged through the bag.

"Any other cash in this place?" he asked, as his eyes scanned the window.

"I have a little in the drawer here but not much. I don't—"

"Shut up, and give it to me." He took the money out of her wallet and threw her purse at her as Grace took out what cash she had, around eighty pounds, and handed it to him. He grabbed it out of her hands and left the shop.

Grace locked the shop door, ran up the stairs to her office and called the police from her cell phone. She stood there, breathing heavily, unsure of what to do next. Crossfield Books was now added to the growing list of burglaries committed on the block.

Grace went back down the stairs to the kitchen and waited for the police. Her legs felt rubbery, and she couldn't stop the trembling in her hands. Coffee was spilled everywhere, even on the ceiling and her favorite mug, the one Wesley bought her that read, 'I like big books, and I cannot lie,' lay broken on the wood floor.

That's how her day from hell ended. It didn't start out much better...

The bell on the door announced a customer, finally. Grace got up from her desk and looked to the bookstore floor below. Unfortunately, it was not a customer. It was her landlord.

"Hi, Mr. Resnik," she called. She tried to sound pleased to see him, but in truth, he always made her feel uneasy with his wandering eyes.

"Hi, Grace. Bring that pretty face down here a minute. I need a word." He was a short, stout man, balding, and Grace noticed that he always had an odd smell about him, like a long-forgotten closet.

Grace made her way down from the upstairs loft that held her office. The winding, wrought iron staircase that led to her bookshop below was one of her favorite elements of the space. It reflected the Georgian era of the building, simple and uniform, not yet influenced by the more detailed Gothic Revival style.

She rented the store from Mr. Armin Resnik as well as a small flat above. He owned the whole block of little shops and apartments in the magnificent eighteenth century building. Along with Grace's bookstore, there were a couple of offices, a hearing center, a thrift store, and a coffee shop that was run by Grace's close friend Devita and her family. She had been warned early on to be wary of Mr. Resnik, one of the tenants even referred to him as a first-class sleaze ball.

At the bottom of the stairs, Grace accidentally dropped her water bottle. She bent down to pick it up and bumped heads with him as he had also bent down to get it. An unpleasant mix of garlic and sweat offended her nose.

"Allow me, sweetheart," he said with a grin. His face had a permanent sneer, and his eyes were always shifting under half-shut lids. She was suddenly glad she'd opted for the high-buttoned blouse this morning.

"What brings you 'round?" she asked, moving away from him. "I've just brewed some fresh coffee. Care for a cup?" She headed for the back room, in a rush to put some distance between them.

"No, thank you," he was picking his teeth with his tongue. "I'm afraid I'm making my rounds this morning to tell you that I'm going to have to raise the rents again."

"What? Oh no. Another increase?" She'd spent most of the morning in her office working on the books, which looked bleak, as usual. Her bookstore meant everything to her. She had fulfilled a lifelong dream when she opened it. Unfortunately, something always needed repairing in the old shop, and in her tiny flat. She was already behind in her bills; higher rent would really sting. "You can't do that, Mr. Resnik. You'll put me out of business." She felt warmth rise under her collar, her hands began to sweat, and she was sure her face was turning red. She tried to hold eye contact with him and remain assertive, even though her body was giving her insecurity away. All her life, when Grace experienced stress, it revealed itself to the world.

He put his hairy hands on his broad hips. He always wore the same clothes: a yellowing collared shirt and gray polyester slacks. His pants were too long for his short, stocky legs and pooled around his brown penny loafers.

"The lease states that if repairs are of a safety concern, I have the right to obtain money from shop owners. Have you looked at the eaves, Grace? Dangerous. They're going to fall on someone's head one of these days. You wouldn't want a lawsuit, would you?"

"No, of course not. I'll figure something out." *Yeah, right,* she thought. What was there to figure out? She was in trouble and right now couldn't see a way out of it.

"Mind if I use the loo? The wife's coffee always runs right through me."

Grace stood there, absolutely depressed and discouraged. She looked around at her beloved bookstore with its many collections and rare editions.

She knew she'd probably never get wealthy selling books; that was never her goal. She just wanted to make a decent living surrounded by everything she loved. She enjoyed her regular clientele, who also appreciated the architecture of the space, with its creaky floors and quaint, comfy alcoves.

Grace scrimped and saved to decorate the bookstore with a sensitivity to the period: dark wood, curvilinear chairs, patterned oriental rugs on the stone floor, antique tables and sideboards. She had collected some Imari style table lamps from an estate sale as well as oil paintings and portraits that added to the ambiance of the tidy little shop.

She'd made use of all the rooms in the place that was originally a private home in 1724. Rumors had circulated about the original owner haunting the dining room, the largest room with a fireplace, and that brought customers in as well. Her assistant, Wesley, had the idea of placing the Bloods and Penny Dreadfuls in there and she noticed it had boosted those sales somewhat.

The life she built herself here in England, with her store and a few close friends, was the happiest of all her thirty-four years. She had made her dream of opening a bookshop a reality, and there was no way she was losing it. She had even started on her first manuscript. All her life, she longed to see her name on the spine of a book. Finding the time to write when you had your own business was difficult though, especially with the constant upkeep of the old building.

The bathroom door opened, and Mr. Resnik walked out, still in the process of pulling up his fly.

He walked toward the door and without turning around, she heard him mutter, "I'll expect an extra one-eighty on your check for November."

Grace straightened a crooked line of books, "I don't

know how I'm going to come up with it, but I guess I'll have to try."

He stopped short of the door and took a survey of the wall and ceiling. Without looking at Grace, he said, "By the way, your toilet wouldn't flush. You see what I mean, dear. The old place needs some TLC and TLC costs money."

That's just great, thought Grace, wanting to throw up. She felt relieved that he left before he noticed any other costly issues but was crushed by the news of another increase. Not to mention another problem with her toilet and having to deal with whatever he left behind in there.

She slumped to the small kitchen and poured herself a coffee, racking her brain for ideas to cut more corners. She couldn't lose her little shop. She'd come so far, done so well, all on her own.

Her family back in Scotland had money. She couldn't ask them, though; she'd left on bad terms long ago.

She hadn't seen or spoken to her mother or sister in almost eighteen years; ever since she left for boarding school and later to attend business school in England. She'd paid for that all on her own, working two jobs and living in shared housing. She had sent letters to her mother, she did miss her, even though there was a lot of resentment. But she never heard back. Some were returned unopened.

After her father's disappearance, she'd had no reason to stay and put up with her sister's poor treatment of her any longer. Fourteen years of abuse and torment was long enough. Morvin was much older than Grace and held power over her with master manipulation. Her sister had a talent for pushing things to the limit and then drawing back the torture. She'd pull out Grace's hair or pinch and bite her, but leave no deep marks or blood.

"Oh, Gracie," her mother would say, "stop your bubbling. Your sister's just teasing. It's how she says she loves you."

Grace resented the fact that her parents, especially her mother, let the abuse continue and never took her tears seriously. So, Grace went off to boarding school soon after and, since then, had only spoken to her Aunt Lena, her mother's sister, a few times.

Coffee in hand, Grace headed back to her office to face her red numbers again. That's when she had let out a scream and dropped her cup as the hooded man grabbed her from behind.

"Well, could've been my neck that's broken instead," she said, as she picked up the broken pieces. Tears began streaming down her face. "What a bloody day." She was just about to add 'what next?' when she heard the toilet begin to run.

CHAPTER TWO

"NOW, WHAT DID that customer want?" Grace looked down at the order sheet. "Oh yeah, a first edition *The Far Pavilions*." She scanned her store inventory list. "Aha. I do have one. Let's see, where are you?" She walked to the back wall, where some of her hard copies were stored.

The trauma of the robbery was still raw, but she was beginning to put it behind her. The fact that the police had apprehended the young thief that very afternoon certainly helped. Staying busy in her beloved bookstore also kept her mind occupied and away from replaying the scene continuously in her mind.

After putting herself through business school, Grace worked her way up the ranks and eventually became a regional sales manager for one of the larger bookstore chains in Britain. Within a few years, she'd saved enough money to pay the deposit on this little gem—a bookstore in an immensely charming eighteenth-century building.

Books seemed to belong in an old building. The mystery held between the covers should be stored in a space with mystery as well. Books, especially antique books, belonged with creaky floors, sculpted archways, and labyrinthine corridors. A bookshop needed to smell of nineteenth-century pulp paper, decayed bindings and the settled dust of centuries past. Grace still found herself intoxicated by those aromas every time she walked through her front door.

She worked hard for her little business, never turning much, if any, profit. But Grace felt her life was abundant because she was doing it on her own, and doing what she loved.

"There you are." She spied the thick volume way up on the top shelf. "Figures." She sighed loudly and grabbed the nearby library ladder. She tucked a strand of her curly brown hair behind an ear and kicked off her heels. She climbed up to the sixth step and steadied herself with one hip, resting it on a rung then shimmied the heavy book out with her left hand until it was almost ready to fall. With one more nudge, she let the book land heavily on her chin, and then fall to her chest, where she could manage to raise her right shoulder and bicep high enough to secure it. She then safely grabbed it with her trustworthy left hand.

"I saw that. Why don't you ask for help?" asked Wesley from below.

"I managed, didn't I?" answered Grace, feeling the warmth of a welt beginning to form on her chin. Grace had been born with Erb's Palsy in her right arm, a disability caused by traumatic birth. It caused her right arm to have limited movement and weakness, and it was also slightly smaller than her left. Although it sometimes made everyday tasks difficult and caused her frequent pain, she had never let it stop her. Managing a large corporation—no problem; zipping up her coat—challenging. Over the years, Grace became good at hiding her disability. She never expected, nor wanted sympathy and rarely asked for help. Most people, unless they were highly observant, never even noticed it.

"I didn't want to keep you from fixing the toilet," Grace said, as she wriggled back into her shoes.

"Can't be fixed by me, I'm afraid," he said, "We need a plumber. How are you doing anyway, Grace? After the whole break-in thing. Why didn't you just 'Kung Fu' his ass?"

"It's not Kung Fu, Wesley, its kickboxing, and I don't know. It all happened so fast. I guess I didn't get an opportunity. A plumber?" Grace wanted to change the subject. "I don't have money for that, Wesley." Grace was hoping it was going to be an easy fix. She didn't want to give Mr. Resnik any reason to raise the rents again, but the old building did need so much work. Yes, the architecture and character were gorgeous, but it did come with its headaches. He kept raising the rents to pay for much-needed repair and maintenance but really, she didn't see much getting done. One of his big plans that was going to 'cost us all a fortune' was to reface the old building completely. Grace was dead set against this; she preferred restoration instead of refacing.

"I'll pay for the plumber. Just pay me double next month. I can handle it, no problem," said Wesley. "And use whatever's left to change that stupid name on the storefront."

"Oh, my goodness. Again, Wesley? I don't see what's so bad about Crossfield Books. I mean, I guess it's a little boring, but we are in Crossfield, England." Grace began descending the ladder. "Anyway, no, Wes. I already owe you some back pay." She misstepped the last rung; thankfully Wesley caught her arm before she fell. She smiled at him in thanks. "I'll figure something out," she seemed to be saying that a lot lately. "You're so sweet, though." She knew Wesley would work in her store for free if she asked him.

He loved old books and literature almost as much as she, although he also had a passion for graphic novels, something that held no interest for her. He had talked her into selling a few editions that he claimed contained 'serious literary themes and sophisticated artwork.' She had to admit they sold well. Now the genre had a whole section at the back of the store and Wesley was in full charge of it.

"I've been thinking about cool names for the store again, though," he said. How about 'The Raven and Glass Classical Bookstore,' or 'The Dusty Shelf?'" Wesley followed her to the front desk. "Hey, this is a good one—I thought of it while I was playing D & D last night with Josh, 'The Iron Key.' He spread one hand in a long line in front of him as he said it and then looked at Grace with a proud smile.

"Okaayy," Grace drawled. "Those are worse than last time, except for the second one. I kind of like that. And it suits this place—take a look at those cobwebs in that corner." She gave him a wink.

Grace sounded light and cheery, but in actuality, she was in real danger of losing her little shop. With ever-increasing high rent and the poor condition of the old place, she was beginning to sink fast. It killed her to think of losing everything she'd worked so hard for, everything she loved. Failure would be crushing, especially when she'd done so much, all on her own, with no help from her wealthy family.

"Maybe Marc will be able to fix the toilet," she said. Marc was Wesley's older brother and Grace's boyfriend.

"Oh please," he replied, "if I can't fix it, what makes you think Prince Charming can?"

The two brothers were like honey and lemons, in manner and appearance. Wesley was the younger of the two by eight years. He was heavyset with a round, pleasant face, still marked with adolescence even though he was in his early twenties. He had a gentle nature and a soft heart.

Marc, on the other hand, was tall and lean, with a chiseled chin and prominent features. Everywhere they went, women followed him with their eyes, and he knew it. He was charismatic and sophisticated. Too bad you couldn't mix the two brothers and have the perfect man.

Marc wasn't Grace's type, but he pursued her so romantically, leaving flowers at the door in the mornings, wining and dining her, sending sweet texts on her phone. He'd even quoted some of her favorite authors to impress her.

Wesley always told her she could, and should, do better, but Grace felt the pressure of getting older. She'd dated here and there, never had trouble finding dates, was an attractive woman, but she grew tired of the cycle of meeting someone, getting to know them and then finding out weeks later, they're no match.

Grace had difficulty getting comfortable enough for intimacy. It took time for her, and most of the men she was meeting weren't willing to wait. Her disability, although not easily noticeable, along with some visible, deep scarring on her back, also from childhood, made closeness complicated. She'd managed to get past this stage with Marc, and, to be honest, she found herself swept away by his successful lifestyle, charming smile, and handsome looks.

The one thing the Foster brothers did have in common though: they were both quite handy and intelligent. Marc just happened to be a little wiser in some areas because he was older.

"I don't care who fixes it," Grace continued. "We just need our customers to be able to use it."

"Well, I replaced the flap and checked the chain, maybe we need a whole new toilet. Maybe you and Marc can have a romantic date at the home store, picking up a new shitter," Wesley laughed. "I can picture Mr. Debonair now...impressing you with his vast knowledge of all things potty. Gross. Things still getting serious for you and 'the playa?'" He held his hands up in quotations.

"I don't know. Things are going well, I think." Grace couldn't help but smile a little as she thought of their last date. Marc had slowed down purposely as they passed the jewelers on their walk after dinner.

"You know, Wes, you're are an awesome guy, with so much to offer. Lisa is interested in you. You should ask her out. The four of us could double."

"Oh yeah, and have her compare me to 'Apollo' all night? No, thanks." He kicked his runner into the floor.

"Oh, Wesley," Grace said. She lifted his chin so she could look him right in his big, doe eyes. "If I were ten years younger, Lisa would have to fight me for you. You're the warmest, smartest, funniest guy I've ever known. Seriously, you should be beating them off with a stick." She kissed him on the cheek and ruffled his slightly greasy, curly brown hair. "I mean it, buddy, you're a keeper."

"Yeah, right. You're just saying that," he said, embarrassed. "But let's get real here. You would have to be at least *twenty* years younger." He ducked out of the way just in time, and Grace missed him with a light kick to his ample, denim-sagging rear end.

"Anyway," said Wesley, "Marc is a total jerk. Don't get your hopes up too high. I'm telling you."

"I appreciate your looking out for me, but Marc told me all about his many past relationships. He's honest with me. I think this time might be different for him."

"Ugh, I think I'll go work on the toilet rather than discuss the details of my brother's love life," he said, as he headed to the back. "Don't say I didn't warn you though."

"Yeah, yeah. And for the umpteenth time too."

Indeed, Wesley was the sweetest guy on earth, and she was so grateful to have him in her life.

CHAPTER THREE

THE RAIN WAS teeming down sideways as rain always did in the little town of Crossfield, just outside of Newcastle. It never came in a light drizzle, ever a deluge. Grace ran for cover under a store overhang. Devi joined her, laughing uncontrollably, because Grace almost tripped, running across the street.

"Oh my God, Grace, that would have been freakin' priceless." She was bent over, still in hysterics, trying to catch her breath. "For someone named Grace, you sure aren't very graceful."

The two had just finished their weekly kickboxing class. Grace had eventually relented to go with Devi after weeks of constant hounding. With frequent break-ins on the block she explained that they should both know how to protect themselves, just in case. Grace reluctantly gave in but now found she actually enjoyed the classes and looked forward to them. They had been going for almost eight weeks now, and Grace was really getting good. The instructor always commented on her powerful right kick, which was probably due to the daily running Grace had kept up for the past few years; a habit she fell in love with after realizing that staying thin after thirty might be tricky for her 5'3" frame.

Grace was grateful Devi didn't mention the robbery to the instructor. She felt stupid enough as it was that she hadn't adequately defended herself, but practicing in the safety of the class was a whole lot different than using it in a real life situation.

"Wouldn't have been so funny if I'd have face planted and then been run over by a bus though, would it?" Grace couldn't help but start giggling as well as she imagined how funny she must've looked trying to save herself from slamming head-first onto the sidewalk.

Devi laid a hand on Grace's shoulder, finally calming down. "It's your turn for lunch Gracey, right?" she said, as they walked the short block to the restaurant. The little Italian place had the best pasta salad, and their pizzas were cooked authentically in a brick oven; Grace and Wesley often shared a pie on Friday nights after closing. It was just a few blocks from Grace's bookstore, just before the financial district of Crossfield, where the buildings began to lose that Old World charm.

"What? I don't think so. I paid last time. Remember your chicken was a little pink, so you ripped the waiter's head off." Grace winked at her. Devi was so easy to rile up.

"I did not rip his head off, but I'd have liked to have

strangled whoever cooked the damn thing. Could've killed me, you know. Anyway, forget it, I'll pay. I'm definitely not arm wrestling you for it. You almost ripped my arm off last time." Grace's left arm was extraordinarily strong as it had to do the job of two.

Grace gave a light fist pump. "*Yes!*"

They approached the doorway and took a minute to shake the rain off. Devi peered in the window, checking for vacant tables.

"The restaurant looks busy," she said. Devi suddenly turned serious and started pushing Grace's shoulder, trying to move her forward.

"What are you doing? What's wrong?" Grace asked, alarmed by her friend's behavior.

Devi continued to try to push Grace along. "Nothing, let's just go. It's too busy."

"Devi stop. It's always busy." Grace looked inside the restaurant for herself. "What's the prob—" then she saw it, or rather, saw them. Inside, against the wall, in a cozy, candlelit corner, sat her boyfriend, Marc. He wasn't alone. Across from him sat a pretty young woman, smiling and holding his hand. Any thoughts that Grace's mind might try inventing to excuse the meeting were quickly dashed when she saw Marc bring the woman's hand to his mouth and kiss it while he fondly gazed into her eyes.

"What a bastard," said Devi. "Let's go."

Grace almost banged on the glass, but anger mixed quickly with heartbreak, and instead, she took her friend's advice. Better to have a plan in place than fly off the handle and end up embarrassing herself.

They ran the two blocks to Devita's café, and while

Grace took a seat at the counter and removed her drenched jacket, Devi poured two big glasses of Merlot.

She handed Grace her glass, "I'm so sorry, hon. Wesley's always saying what a player he is."

"I know." Grace took a large swig and swallowed hard through the big swell in her throat. "I just thought this was special. I thought I was the one that was settling him down, you know? I'm so stupid."

"Stop that, Grace. You are not stupid. *He* is definitely stupid, taking an awesome lady like you for granted. He doesn't deserve you."

"Thanks, Devi. Better to find out now, I guess." She guzzled the rest of her wine, wanting to go home, be alone, and drown her sorrows. "I'm gonna go. I'll call you later, okay?"

"Hang on, girlfriend." Devi went to the back, to the kitchen, and returned a few seconds later with a tub full of *kulfi*, a traditional Indian ice cream. "Take this with you. It'll help."

Thank goodness for Devi. She really was a great friend, a great person.

Grace had come to Church Street three years ago to view a space to let, which soon after became her bookstore. After meeting with Mr. Armin Resnik, she had come to Spice Chai, Devi's family-owned café, and ordered some tea. The aromas coming from the kitchen had Grace's mouth watering instantly. The scents of curry sauces with onions, tomatoes, garlic, and ginger were heavenly, and the décor inside the little café was rustic and charming with hues of deep, rich reds and golds. There was soft

Indian music playing in the background and loud voices coming from the busy kitchen.

Devi had brought Grace the hot cup of tea herself that day and then proceeded to talk Grace's head off. She acted as if they were old friends, not complete strangers. Devi went on about exasperating husbands, cold English weather, the state of the roads; you name it. She wasn't annoying, though, not in the least. Grace felt immediately like a regular patron; like she belonged, and she was thankful for it. Devi spoke enthusiastically with her slender hands, her fingers long and graceful. Her large, chocolate-colored eyes were captivating with thick, sweeping black lashes that blinked dramatically.

This was a new town for Grace; hopefully, the beginning of a good life and a successful business. New friends were just what she needed. She didn't know it then, but they would become the best of friends; kindred spirits.

Devi and her husband, Manny, had opened the café five years previously. Along with the usual café fare: coffees, teas, muffins, and pastries, they also offered authentic Indian dishes made by Devi and her mother; the best Indian take away in Crossfield, possibly the whole of Northern England. Grace's favorite was the mixed vegetables, extra spicy, with garlic Naan.

Grace walked toward the door with her tub of ice cream. She felt Devi's long arms wrap around her from behind.

"Make sure you call me, Gracey, I'll worry."

"You're the best, Devi," she said. "I will."

Grace strolled to her apartment in the rain. She didn't care about getting soaked; this way, no one on the street would notice her tears. She came across familiar faces, nodded hello as she passed, but she was not really seeing them at all. She was hurt, betrayed, and right pissed off.

She approached the door to her building but kept on walking. She picked up her speed a little and headed for the park where she usually took her morning runs. She put her ice cream down on a bench and then proceeded to the park path at a sprint.

How could she be so stupid? He really had her fooled. What an idiot she'd been. Her speed increased as she went over things in her mind. Her feet flew over the pavement, leaving a trail of anger and hurt behind her.

That girl he was with is so young too, and so pretty. Is that why he cheated? Because I'm getting old and maybe not as firm or perky as that little whore. Oh, stop it, Grace. It's not her fault. She'll probably end up hurt by him too.

She was alone at the park; apparently, everyone else had sense enough to stay out of the cold rain. She tried to ignore the frigid drops as they mixed with her warm tears. She was running as fast as she could now, trying to outrun her thoughts and her grief.

Her lungs eventually felt like they might burst, so she had to stop. She bent over and placed her hands on her knees. On her final large exhale she let out an anguished, angry roar. It felt great to let go and release the emotion, but she probably looked like a lunatic. She turned and jogged at a light pace, back to the start of the path, and picked up her ice cream as she passed it.

Back in front of her building, she noticed Gus, the homeless man who was always collecting bottles in her neighborhood. Grace always gave him her spare change when she had it, and sometimes she would make an extra sandwich in the morning for him and hand it to him when he passed by the bookstore. He was a nice man, down on his luck, and Grace knew, at any time, any of us could end up in the same state.

"Hi, Gus," she said.

"Hello, Miss Grace."

"How're you going to stay dry tonight?" she asked him.

"Gotta spot at the shelter, ma'am. Suzie's holding it for me," his tongue sometimes slipped out through his missing front teeth when he talked.

"Well, here," she handed him the tub of ice cream. "Share this with her when you get there. My treat."

"Uh, thank you, Miss Grace. She loves ice cream." Suzie was a social worker who volunteered at the shelter and really took a shine to old Gus.

"You're welcome. Better get going before the doors close for the night."

He tipped his worn hat to her, and she entered her apartment building. Sometimes it took someone like Gus to put your problems in perspective.

"Up yours, Marc," she said as she turned the key to her flat. Ernie was there at the door with his usual loud feline greeting. "I've got my Ernie waiting for me, and he loves me, young or old." She picked him up in her arms and hugged him, then went to the cupboard for her wineglass.

CHAPTER FOUR

GRACE SAT DOWN at her desk with a stack of unopened mail. She rubbed her temples, trying to ease the effects of too much sorrow drowning the night before. The pile of her usual late payment notices, past dues, and final warnings weren't helping her head at all.

"What's this?" It was a letter from a legal firm in Scotland.

Dear Ms. Calhoun,

We regret to inform you of your mother's failing health. It is of utmost importance that you return home to your family's estate as we expect her imminent passing. Margaret has requested your presence, not only to say final words, but also to inform you of the final arrangements. Please let our office know immediately upon your arrival.

Sincerely,
Jackson Humbly
Senior Partner, HD&F Law
32 Winston Row, Glasgow

"Oh, my God. My mother's dying." She stood up and went to the small window, the only window in her tiny loft office. Painted shut long ago, it couldn't be opened, and you could barely see through it after centuries of wind, weather, and dust.

The sun peeking over the horizon gave a rare, but welcome, warm glow to the quiet street. Grace's little office was always quite dark, even on the sunniest of days, so she had collected a few lamps to help light up the room. Her favorite was the Emeralite banker's lamp that sat on the corner of her desk. From 1916, it still worked, had the original pull chain and gave an eye-pleasing illumination from the green glass shade. Along with her scattered, eclectic lamp collection, Grace had many candles situated around the room. The effect when lit, was warm, cozy.

She liked her office. It made dealing with her money problems a little less stressful and gave her a private spot to work on the logistics of running her business. The loft was small but homey. Grace had adorned the room with an oriental area rug, a small antique desk, and select artwork. She especially liked the fact that she could see the bookstore floor from the loft's balcony.

Grace thought about the last time she had seen her mother.

She left her family home in Scotland at only sixteen. Her Aunt Lena made all the arrangements for her to attend boarding school. Then, after achieving scholarships, she moved to Manchester University in England. Grace vowed never to return home, having suffered many years of physical and mental torment at the hand of her older sister, Morvin. Add the fact that her mother never punished

Morvin for her evil deeds, and most of the time didn't even believe Grace, made her eager to get far away and try to build a life of her own. It had taken years and a lot of self-growth to overcome her feelings of being stupid and useless. How many times did she have to hear that she was just an accident waiting to happen? But she had overcome it and become much stronger (although a stubborn tendency toward slipping, tripping, and spilling remained). Seeing this letter from home, however, brought back all those feelings of when she was that scared, self-conscious young girl.

Grace remembered how much her mother had argued with her during that last week at home. She insisted on going to boarding school and her mother insisted that she was doing no such thing. So, Grace ended up leaving without her blessing. She often replayed that moment, of looking back at her mother's face as the taxi drove away, and recalled that her mother's expression revealed anger more than sadness. She also remembered that Morvin wasn't there to see her off; she probably could not have been happier at finally being rid of 'silly little Grace, such a sad waste of space.'

Now she's supposed to return? But too much damage had been done. So much time had passed. She'd worked so hard to change from that self-conscious, damaged girl into the self-sufficient, hard-working woman she was now.

Grace looked over at her favorite painting: a gorgeously framed Van Gogh reproduction of *Poppies and Butterflies*. She rewarded herself with it years ago, with the first paycheck she received as an Inventory Analyst at a large chain bookstore; pleased that she was finally putting her business degree to use.

In the eighteen years since she'd left home, she'd sent a few birthday cards to her mother and a letter or two, when she found herself missing her family home, and her mother and father. She never received one reply, not one birthday card or Christmas card since she left. That hurt Grace deeply. She always hoped for a letter of apology, for the way they let Morvin treat her, but they had been blind to her lies and manipulation.

How could her mother shut her out so completely? Maybe because she was angry at her for leaving, but things had gotten so much worse after Grace's father disappeared, and she couldn't take it anymore. Her sister told her their father ran away because he couldn't stand looking at Grace's hideous, deformed arm and because of the heavy burden it put on the whole family. Grace knew that wasn't true. Father was always telling her she could do anything anyone else could do.

She moved closer to the painting and smiled as she recalled a rare moment with her father. He was never home much, but when he was he had always been kind and encouraging. He would never let her dwell on her disability; in fact, he barely acknowledged it.

She had to concentrate now to remember his face. The years were slowly erasing it from her memory, like an old, fading photograph. She did, however, remember his eyes, particularly on that one day in the summer, when Grace was about six or seven. Father took her fishing with him for the day. It was a gorgeous, perfectly warm afternoon and he had been teaching her to fly-fish, off the bank of a river. He looked down at her, the deep blue sky behind him, and she remembered thinking it was as if his eyes were just holes and she could see the blue of the sky right through them.

Her father had noticed a wounded butterfly, struggling in the grass; its right wing was damaged. They watched as it struggled but then eventually managed to take flight and flit away across the river. Father said that, just like that butterfly, she too could overcome any obstacle with the same determination. He told her about the changes a butterfly undergoes in its short life, and this teaches us about the importance of going through those changes with grace (she remembered him tickling her under her chin as he said the word) and lightness. "That's you, Gracey...my little flutterby."

Grace sighed deeply and walked back to her desk. She took a sip of her coffee and grimaced as the lukewarm liquid met her lips. She drank some anyway.

How could she go back now? Back to that enormous mansion with its many rooms holding terrible secrets and silent sufferings. Back to seeing her awful sister and being belittled and subjected again to her abuse. She just wouldn't. Morvin can handle it all. She would, once again, just push it from her mind, press it way back there along with all the other vile memories and continue with her life.

Grace sat down and tried to focus again on paperwork, her mound of bills; deciding which ones to pay now, which ones could wait a little longer. But her mind kept spinning; returning home, where her mother was ailing, and then she'd find herself thinking about Marc, that cheating bastard. What would she say to him when he called? If he called?

She reached for her now cold coffee. It slipped from her grasp and spilled all over her desk, her bills, everything.

"Shit, shit, shit." Grace stood up quickly before the cold, brown river poured onto her lap. "What a week from hell," she said. She rubbed at her temples again.

CHAPTER FIVE

"HOW LONG WOULD you be gone? A week? Two? Big Deal. Wesley and I can handle the store." Devi was trying to convince Grace to make the trip back home. "We did fine when Marc took you to Spain." Wesley and Grace stopped by Devi's café after closing the bookstore, which they regularly did. The coffee shop was relatively quiet now, the dinner rush long passed.

"Did you really have to bring him into the conversation?" Grace was still fuming mad at Marc. He'd called twice since she saw him at the restaurant but she couldn't bring herself to talk to him yet. *Let him stew in his guilt for a while longer,* she thought.

"Sorry, but that is another good point. After what Marc did, a change of scenery might be good for you." Devi sipped her coffee.

Grace ran her fingers roughly through her hair and let out a loud sigh.

"I agree with Devi, Grace," said Wesley. Devi always gave Wesley extra whip on his hot chocolate, and he was wearing half of it on his upper lip. He did it on purpose to try and make Grace laugh. He didn't like seeing her down and stressed out. "What if there's a large inheritance? You sure could use some money to fix up the store. And... ahem, get a new sign," he added under his breath.

"I don't want my family's money, Wesley. I told you that." She snickered a little and handed him a napkin. "I would like to say goodbye to my mum, though, and I'd love to see my aunt too, but I hate the thought of seeing Morvin. It's taken me all these years to recover from the damage she did to my self-esteem. I'm afraid she'll bring all those feelings back."

"No way," said Devi. "You're a completely different person now. I think it will be therapeutic for you to face her as the successful woman you are and show your sister that you're worth something, that you matter. Can you imagine the look on her face when she sees how beautiful and strong you've become?"

"What about Ernie? I can't just leave him on his own." Ernie was Grace's six-year-old tabby cat.

"I'll look after the fat, beady-eyed little monster," said Wesley. "Sodded thing loves me anyway." Whenever Wesley was over the cat would not stay off his lap. Ernie would knead his claws into Wesley's legs, get comfortable, and then, at any sudden noise, jump off, leaving bloody scratches behind and scaring Wesley half to death. Grace always found it quite entertaining.

Grace shifted in her chair and looked down at her empty cup. She felt sick to her stomach all of a sudden. "I'm going to the washroom."

"I'll get us some more coffee," said Devi.

"My hot chocolate needs a refill too, Dev," said Wesley.

She clicked her tongue at him and grabbed his cup, muttering something under her breath as she walked toward the counter.

"What's that, Devi? I can't understand your grumbling." Wesley snickered as she continued her mumbling, only now she was doing it louder.

A few minutes later, a tired and puffy-eyed Grace returned and sat down next to Wesley.

"These are all good points, you know," Wesley continued, "and also if you go and then find that it's too much, turn around and come home again. At least you won't have any regrets about not saying your goodbyes. That's the main thing, right?"

"It is a five-hour drive, you know, Wes. It's not just down the block." The drive back to Craigrook House, her family's estate, would be a long one, through mostly country roads. It was too early in the season for snow, thank goodness, but she hoped her old 1973 Volkswagen was up to the task.

Grace knew all their points were valid, and she knew she probably should go back, but, although she'd confided a few stories of her difficult childhood, her two friends didn't even know the half of it. Would they still suggest she go if they knew everything?

Loud voices started from the kitchen as Devi walked out with the drinks on a tray. There were a few other customers in the café but, just like Grace and Wesley, they were regulars and were used to Devi and her mother's loud bickering back and forth in Hindi. It always sounded like they were mad as hell at each other, but they usually weren't. Devi's mother didn't speak much English. She knew 'hello,' 'goodbye' and 'not good.' A waving finger always accompanied the latter.

"You guys seriously think I should go?" asked Grace, silently praying that they might give her a reason not to.

The two looked at each other and at the same time said, "Yes!"

"Well, there it is. I guess I'm going. Oh my god, I can't believe I just said that."

"Ooh, Gracey," came a voice from behind them. It was Aanandi, Devi's mother, shuffling along slowly toward their table in bright blue slippers. She took Grace's chin in her small, cold, wrinkled hand and looked into her face, then proceeded to speak to Grace gently in Hindi.

Devi translated, "My dear little Grace. Be strong and know that we are with you, here and here, always." She pointed to Grace's heart and forehead. In her other hand was a large pastry, still warm from the oven. She handed it to Grace. "Mmm, mmm." She made a gesture with her own hands toward her mouth and smiled at Grace. Devi continued to translate. "You don't need that terrible man in your life anyway. He is no good for you. You will find another soon, a better one." Then came the finger as she said in English, "Not good, not good."

Wesley couldn't help but snicker as did Devi. Aanandi gave them both stern looks and then hugged Grace and shuffled away, back into the kitchen. The three of them laughed, in kindness, at the caring older woman's personality. Grace adored Devi's mother and envied their relationship. Devi was lucky to have her.

"Well, if I'm going, you guys, I'll need something stronger than coffee here," said Grace.

"Two Cosmos, coming right up!" said Devi, excited, as she got up from the table.

"Ahem," said Wesley.

"Ugh... three."

"How am I going to leave you two? You'll be at each other throats within mere hours."

"We promise to behave," said Wesley, "don't we, Devinator?"

Devi called over to them from the bar. "At least until you get back."

Grace laughed and noticed that she was mindlessly biting at her knuckle, something she hadn't done in years.

"Oh, God, don't look...Marc's coming," said Devi, averting her gaze from the doorway a little too obviously. She practically ran from the table to the kitchen.

"Oh no," Grace didn't know what to do. She fixed her hair.

"I'm outta here," said Wesley.

"Gee thanks, friends," said Grace sarcastically.

He walked into the café and directly over to Grace. "Hi, babe. You haven't been returning my calls. What's up?"

My God, he looked good. Dressed impeccably, as usual, right down to his polished, designer, monk strap shoes. "Where's your jailbait...oh, sorry, I mean new girlfriend?"

"What are you talking about, Gracey?" he flicked back his hair and smiled, then leaned in and touched her hand.

"I saw you, Marc. At Dimitris, getting very close with Hannah Montana." *That was a good one,* she thought, as she drew her hand away.

"What? You were there?" he sat back in the chair. His eyes widened, and he looked around the room, searching for a quick excuse.

"Don't worry about it. I'm just glad I found out what everyone always says about you is correct. I'm over it." Grace got up to leave, but he grabbed her arm.

"Gracey, don't be so rash. It was nothing. One of the guys at work fixed it up. I didn't like her. She has nothing on you. You're so...so much more...mature."

Grace couldn't believe what he said. What a complete ass. He continued, "I've fallen for you, gorgeous. You make me feel complete. I thought we had something. Don't throw it away. I need you."

"Marc, I'm leaving town for a while," she pulled her arm sharply out of his grasp. "Maybe we'll talk when I get back. But right now, you repulse me." She put her bag over her shoulder and said goodbye to Devi before walking out the door. She didn't look back at him; she wouldn't dare give him the satisfaction and ruin her perfect exit.

Perhaps, deep down, she always knew he wasn't the one for her, but she was honestly so tired of going to bed alone. She wanted someone to go home to, someone to grow old with.

CHAPTER SIX

GRACE PICKED OUT some sweaters and a couple of pairs of jeans. She stuffed them into her large over-sized weekender and scanned her tiny bedroom for her warmest wool coat. She was having a lot of trouble picking out her clothes for her trip back home, and had packed, emptied, and re-packed her bag four times already and hadn't even started picking out shoes yet.

She sat down on the edge of her bed, feeling exasperated. She knew her problem wasn't about this outfit or that one; it was about the trip itself. Even though she'd resigned herself to going, she couldn't shake the nervousness in her belly.

"Hey, little man," she said to Ernie as he wound in and out of her legs. She named her cat after her father's favorite author, Ernest Hemingway; he had a full collection of the author's work in his study, including a few first editions. She remembered her father quoted him often. One of his favorites was, 'The world breaks everyone, and afterward, some are strong at the broken places.'

"Dinner time is it, Ernie?" She picked up her cat and went to the kitchen. After a short scan of her empty cupboards, she plucked a single can of tuna. She lifted it in front of Ernie's face as in a toast, "Tonight, we feast, for tomorrow…I go back and face hell." The cat looked at her quizzically. "Never mind, furry face. You get a treat tonight, my friend."

She pierced the tin with the opener, and the meowing started and didn't cease until she placed a small portion in front of him. She prepared the rest as a sandwich for herself, poured a glass of Pinot Noir, and sat on the settee in the living room. Ernie jumped onto her lap before she even had time to settle and began purring as he kneaded her legs into cushiony softness. She pulled up a playlist on her phone, and the smooth sounds of Euge Groove began playing on her Bluetooth speaker.

Grace loved the old bones of the eighteenth-century apartment building. It was painted a clean white and had warm wood floors throughout. After a long day, and sometimes night, of working in her eclectic, slightly cramped bookstore, she would wrestle into her oversized, puffy chesterfield and try to relax. She felt soothed by the warm tones of her carefully picked knickknacks and soft blue accent colors.

Depending on her day and the number of customers she had, she would have either a cup of tea or a large glass of wine; these days there were a lot more empty bottles than there were soggy, pressed tea bags in the bin. Most nights Grace would awaken well into the night, still on the couch, a passing lorry or blaring siren having jolted her awake.

She petted Ernie as he finally settled. "I'm going to miss you, my main man." She took a sip of her wine. "What am I doing, Ernie? What the hell am I thinking?" Ever since she had decided to return home she'd had a constant uneasy feeling in her core. The way you feel just before a job interview or an important meeting.

She wondered if her sister had changed. Maybe the years had softened her. Aunt Lena once mentioned that Morvin had married and had a son. Her husband was a navy man and after only two years decided he preferred living abroad to living with Morvin, and he divorced her. She moved back home to Craigrook and had lived there ever since, caring for their aging mother.

A Summer Night's Dream faded, and the familiar, sexy notes of Kim Waters' *Let's Get On It* filled the room. This particular tune was one of Marc's favorites. She couldn't help smiling as she pictured him swaying to it while he fixed breakfast; the cute way he shook his butt, the taut muscles— "Next," she said and picked another song. She'd never be able to enjoy that awesome song ever again. That sucked; he sucked.

As another song began, Grace's mind returned to her impending trip. She was looking forward to seeing the mansion again. Craigrook House had been in her family since their great-great grandfather purchased it in the late 1800s. It had eleven bedrooms and six bathrooms, three sitting rooms, a parlor, and even a library that her father used as his study.

She did have some good memories of the vast estate from when she was little, with its many servants, cooks, and gardeners. There were lots of guests as well whenever her father was home, which, unfortunately, wasn't very often. When the house was busy, she was less likely to be tormented by her sister.

Thinking back to her bedroom brought a smile to her face, but it faded when she remembered Morvin barging in to torment her or pull her hair or break her toys. Grace was so afraid of Morvin coming into her room that sometimes she would play quietly inside one of the enormous wardrobes. Many times she had silently wished for the back to open into Narnia.

Why did her sister hate her so much? Morvin was always quite somber and introverted, but when it came to Grace she was all of a sudden full of personality, and never in a good way. Grace stayed out of her way, avoided eye contact, and rarely even spoke to her.

Morvin would often push her aside if she passed her in a hallway, or threaten her with violence. 'Wipe that look off your face, or I'll do it for you' was one of Morvin's favorites. She was so sneaky about it, too; never in front of their parents or any other adult for that matter. If Grace's mother ever noticed a welt or a bruise, it was quickly blamed on Grace being accident-prone, which she was.

Well, I'm an adult now. She won't be pushing me around anymore. Grace glugged some more wine. Ernie jumped off her lap when she leaned forward to fill her glass. Maybe she could patch things up with her mother. So much time had passed, they'd all changed, grown. Grace had been angry that her mother always sided with Morvin and never believed Grace when she tried to tell her of the abuse. That anger and hurt may never fully heal, but Grace was a strong woman now, a different person. She had done of lot work on her inner child and part of that work was realizing that her mother, and even Morvin, had inner demons that they too struggled with; everyone did. One of Grace's favorite sayings was, 'Every day we pick our way through unknown territory.' She couldn't remember who said it but it was very accurate. We are all on the same journey through life, and no one has all the answers.

Grace paused the music when she saw her phone light up.

"Hello?"

"Miss Calhoun, please," said a cold voice.

"Speaking."

"Good evening, this is Simon Electric calling, reminding you that you're still in arrears. Your electric service will be interrupted if the full past due amount isn't paid by noon tomorrow."

"But I just paid you forty pounds last week. I made—" Grace was interrupted.

"You must pay the full 'past due' amount. It is long overdue, Miss Calhoun," said the heartless male robot.

"Can I send you half that and then I'll pay the whole thing next Friday?" Grace pleaded.

"I'm afraid this bill's 'past due' portion is no longer negotiable, Miss Calhoun. Have a lovely evening."

"Hello? You did not just hang up on me. Come on." Grace put her head in her hands. "Well, it looks like another cash advance on the old credit card. Just great. And I don't even have the plumbing bill yet." She took another slug of her wine. She patted her lap for Ernie to come back, but he just looked at her and walked away. "Nice, you think I'm a loser as well, do you? Thanks, pal."

The cat meowed at her and flicked his tail as if in agreement.

"I'll only be away for a week or so, Ernie. Wesley will take good care of you. Be nice to him, okay?" The cat looked up at her and the look on his face said, "Yeah, right."

"Well, better get back to packing," Grace said to Ernie, who wasn't paying her any more attention, a clean ass his sudden immediate priority. "After a refill, of course."

CHAPTER SEVEN

GRACE FELT TENSION take root in her shoulders as she drove up the long driveway to Craigrook House. She wasn't sure if it was the long drive that caused her sudden fatigue or the fact that she was about to see her childhood home for the first time in eighteen years. The last time she saw her family home, it was through tears, in the back of a cab, as she vowed never to return.

"Well, here we are." She drew in a deep, shaky breath as she pulled her car around the circular drive and stopped at the front entrance.

Grace sat for a few minutes, looking through the rain-streaked windshield at the mansion where she grew up. The weather was the only thing that looked the same. The last light of day was fading fast, and there was the typical Scottish mist lying low on the ground. However, Grace could see that the once manicured grounds were now overgrown and unkempt.

Dry, brown, skeletal vines were all that remained of the once lush, charming ivy that hugged both sides of the stone-walled entrance. The pretty Scots Rose bushes under the large bow window had become wild, prickly, cruel brambles. Once an inviting, regal façade, it now looked sad, unloved, and melancholy.

Grace covered her head with her bag, locked her car out of habit like she would back home in England, and ran for the cover of the front alcove. She shivered as she pressed a wet finger on the doorbell. The familiar chime rang through the house. She waited a couple of minutes, bouncing from foot to foot to ward off the chill, and then tried the bell again and added a few knocks for good measure. Still no answer. She tried to peer through the window, but the darkness inside revealed nothing.

Grace often asked herself over the last eighteen years why she bothered hanging on to the large brass house key; now she was grateful she had. She tried the key, but it didn't fit. "Just great," she muttered, as the damp cold settled into her bones.

Reluctantly, she decided to check the back entrance, which was quite a distance around the formidable mansion, especially with the surrounding trees and bushes being as overgrown as they were.

The ancient wrought iron gate gave a loud creak of protest as she swung it open and entered the side garden. Her heels got stuck in the cold, wet muck with every step and the large wet bushes that invaded the path on both sides licked at her sleeves, completely drenching them as she went.

After finally clearing the side garden, Grace entered the back patio. She stamped her feet a few times on the concrete in a futile attempt to loosen some of the cold mud from her shoes. She sensed someone watching her from behind and quickly spun around but couldn't see clearly through the misty rain. Was that a person standing over by the hedges?

Grace hurried up the back stairs, slipped and smashed her shin on the top step. She swore under her breath as she righted herself and then quickly tried the doorknob, locked. She raised onto her toes, peeked into the mudroom, and rapped on the door.

"Morvin," she called.

She could have sworn she saw someone moving about inside, but it was hard to see through the patterned sheers. She banged harder and looked again at the hedge behind her. Someone was standing in the downpour looking at her. In the fading light and pouring rain she couldn't make out their features, but they seemed to be wearing a hood, and they were standing at an odd angle, stooped over, like a half-shut knife.

"Hello? Who is that? Is that you, Keaton?" She thought it might be her nephew, Morvin's son. He had to be about eighteen years old now. Aunt Lena told her, the last time they spoke, that Keaton was a bit of a wastrel; no ambition, played video games 24/7 and lived in one of the outbuildings at the back of the estate.

The figure did not reply. Grace continued to pound on the door as the adrenaline kicked in, fueled by her growing fear. If she ran back to her car, she'd have to pass by the person in the shadows, but she couldn't stand out here all night in the freezing rain.

Out of the corner of her eye, she saw something move in the house.

"Morvin! Open the door!" Grace was yelling as she continued pounding, all the while trying to keep watch on the strange figure in the increasing darkness. *What the hell? Why won't she open the damned door?*

Grace once again contemplated running to her car but she was terrified of passing the creep watching her. She took one last look in the window and then, summoning all her courage, tore down the steps, ran past the hooded stranger, and rounded the corner into the muddy side path. In her haste, she slipped again and went down on one knee on the wet, sparse grass and muck. Feeling panic at her back, she chanced a look over her shoulder and saw that the person was still in the same spot. He hadn't followed, but she could see the hood had turned, he was watching her.

Grace darted back through the gate. Her car still looked miles away. She grabbed at her keys as she ran. Her cold, numb, slippery fingers could barely feel them in her grasp. Finally at her car, she unlocked the door and jumped inside. She quickly pushed down all the door locks in a panic, just as a light flickered on in the entrance-way. Grace watched with relief as the large oak front door swung open, and her sister emerged in the doorway.

CHAPTER EIGHT

"THANK GOD YOU'RE home. There's someone out there; scared me half to death. And my key doesn't work. Have the locks been changed?" Grace was out of breath. She peeled off her soaked jacket.

"Hello to you too," Morvin said, as she took Grace's scarf and jacket and hung them on the nearby coat tree, her face expressionless.

"Oh, I'm sorry," Grace smiled at her sister. "Hello, Morvin. It's nice to see you. It's been a long time. You look...good." Grace was a little shocked at her sister's appearance. Yes, she had aged, of course, they both had in the last eighteen years, but apparently, the years had not been at all kind to Morvin.

She had deep, hard lines on her face, and her hair up in a stuffy bun; the once brassy red color now mostly taken over by unruly wires of gray. Her clothes were gray too and matronly, just as they always were; her presence still dark and looming. Grace always called her Lurch from the Addams Family, but never to her face.

"Yes, the locks have been changed. Did you expect everything to remain the same even though you've been absent forever?" Morvin's voice still sounded like she spoke through gravel. *Lurch voice,* thought Grace as she scanned the large foyer and the grand staircase that swept up the left wall and curved at the top to meet the second floor hall.

Everything did look the same as she remembered except for the visible wear and fading of the old furnishings and wallpaper. She noticed inches upon inches of dust that would never have been there when there were servants.

Memories flooded her mind as she stepped into the sitting room to the left of the entranceway. Even the placement of everything was just as she remembered. A familiar standing lamp of brass and rose glass gave a misguided sense of warmth to the room. Grace remembered playing with the lamp's gold cord, pretending the frayed ends were hair in a girl's ponytail. Morvin had a small fire burning in the fireplace, but it didn't seem to be heating the room much. The house was freezing.

Morvin brushed past her, headed toward the kitchen.

"Gee, Grace, nice to see you. How've you been all these years?" Grace muttered sarcastically to herself. She followed Morvin, snapshots of memories flashing in her mind, triggered by the familiar surroundings. She envisioned little Grace skipping through the many rooms, behind her older sister, always trying in vain for Morvin's approval, for her love.

Morvin was thinner than she used to be but was still a large woman, still had the same broad shoulders. "Built like the end of a *hoose*," her father used to say, much to Morvin's chagrin.

"I suppose you'll be wanting tea," Morvin said without looking at Grace.

Well, she hasn't changed a bit, thought Grace. "That'd be lovely, Morvin," she said. "It's freezing outside and honestly not much warmer in here." Grace rubbed her icy hands together and looked around the kitchen, recalling Irene, the short, chubby cook, who was always flushed and harassed, not overly warm or friendly but made the best biscuits and lots of them. Grace remembered giggling as she watched Irene's round rear end shake like crazy as she stirred something on the stove. "Remember Irene's hobnobs?" Grace asked, trying to lighten Morvin's dour mood and make conversation.

"Why are you here...now?" Morvin asked, straight-faced, looking at Grace for the first time.

"For mother, of course. Geez Morvin, sorry if I'm intruding."

"Intruding is exactly what you're doing. We're just fine here. There's no need for you to disrupt your life and come back here." Morvin was trying to open a cookie tin; the strain on her face made her look older than her forty-seven years.

"I'm worried about Mum. I want to be here. Craigrook is my home, too, you know. Here, let me get that." Grace advanced toward Morvin and held out her hand for the tin.

"I said I don't need your help." Morvin gritted her

teeth and strained with all her might but to no avail. The lid did not budge.

"Here, let me," Grace insisted. She grabbed the tin and popped it open, no strain required. Her powerful left arm was no match for any stubborn lid. She handed it back to an annoyed Morvin.

Morvin grumbled slightly and went about plating the biscuits and pouring the tea.

"I noticed you didn't bring any bags. You're not planning on staying here then." Grace wasn't sure if it was a question or a statement.

Morvin banged a cup on the table as Grace took a seat. She wasn't exactly expecting the welcome wagon but hoped that the years might have softened her sister a bit. No such luck, she was still the same, cold, nasty Morvin.

Grace would not be bullied anymore though. She'd suffered plenty as a girl at the hands of her older sister but was not a child any longer.

"I am, yes. My bags are still in the car. I'll stay in my old room. I won't get in your way. I'm staying until our mother is back on her feet. You won't even know I'm here."

"Mother's dead," Morvin said, deadpan, but you could see a faint hint of enjoyment in her eyes as she delivered the horrible news to a shocked Grace.

"What?" Grace said, dumbfounded. "Oh, no. What happened?"

"She had a heart attack through the night. She hadn't been feeling well for some time. You wouldn't know, of course," Morvin said, through thin lips, slightly grinning.

Tears rolled down Grace's cheeks. She didn't get a

chance to say goodbye, to say anything. She couldn't believe it.

"Were you there? Did she say anything?" Grace asked, hoping her mother didn't die alone in the hospital.

"Of course, I was there. I've always been there. Mother died painfully, but it was over fast. She told me she loved me in those last seconds." Morvin looked Grace directly in the eyes and sneered. "She thanked me for being a good daughter. Those were her exact words."

It was clear Morvin wanted to hurt Grace and, as usual, succeeded with a surplus.

After some uncomfortable silence, Grace asked, "Well, what do we do now? What's the first step?" She cupped her tea with her hands, trying to warm them.

"You're not doing a thing, like I said. Maybe you weren't listening. You are not needed here." Morvin walked to the hallway. "Stay the night, if you must, but you can just go back to your stupid little life in the morning."

After Grace had left for England, Morvin always thought Grace would come back, begging at the door for help and forgiveness. When she didn't, and they heard from Aunt Lena that she was doing quite well, Morvin was unpleasantly surprised. It had to be hard, all on her own, with a disability as well. Then Morvin would shrug the thoughts off and surmise that Grace was probably whoring or doing something sleazy like that.

As Morvin walked down the hall, she added, "You know where your room is."

Grace called after her, "Wait a minute, Morvin. We should talk about this." Grace stood, following. "I'm not leaving!" she yelled at Morvin's back.

She sat back down, put her head in her hands and wept, alone, in the kitchen where she once ate warm bowls of porridge, completed homework assignments, and occasionally sat across from her father's curtain of newspaper. Although she recognized her surroundings, remembered the old fridge with its rounded edges and yellow color, the rhythm of the ticking grandfather clock in the hall, it wasn't truly home for Grace, not in the traditional sense. She never felt safe here, another thing that hadn't changed.

She took their full cups to the sink and went to the kitchen door. She looked out the window to see if the strange figure was still lurking outside in the shadows. It was hard to see through the wet darkness, but it appeared whoever it was, was gone.

She had to go back out there, to her car. What if he was out front, waiting for her? *Oh well,* she thought, *I'm not sleeping in the nude in this frigid house.*

On her way to the door, she passed the old telephone desk and grabbed a sharp letter opener, just in case. She noticed a notepad with the lawyer's name on it, Jackson Humbly. It had tomorrow's date: four o'clock.

CHAPTER NINE

I T FELT SO strange to be back in her childhood home after all these years, especially with her mother and father both gone. She peeked into the sitting room. Her mother would have been sitting in the floral high back chair, a cup of tea on the side table, and a crossword in her lap, her half-rimmed glasses sitting on the end of her nose.

"Up to bed, Gracey, don't forget to brush your teeth. Don't bother your father; he's working." She could almost hear her voice coming from the empty chair.

Her father never minded being interrupted by Grace. She would sneak into his study, and he would stop what he was doing and scoop her up for a goodnight kiss. "Off you go, tired little flutterby."

Grace looked over at the large study door. She felt like a child again, wanting to get a goodnight hug from the only person who ever made her feel like she was loved or wanted.

She made her way up the wide winding staircase to the second floor. In total, there were four floors at Craigrook. The kitchen and main living areas were all on the main floor, three bedrooms and two baths made up the second. At the west end of the house was another staircase that led to some more bedrooms and another parlor. There was also a basement at the back of the large home that used to be the servant's quarters and storage rooms. The fourth floor had more storage, her mother's craft room, a gathering space, and access to the rooftop terrace. The house was once grand and majestic, but now it seemed empty, dusty, and sad.

Grace's old bedroom was left of the second-floor staircase and down the end of a long hallway, along with a guest room across the hall and another next door. She peeked inside them and saw that they were still fully furnished, unchanged, and unused. She paused before entering her room, her hand resting on the glass doorknob—so many memories in the little room behind the door, many of them traumatizing.

She took a breath, turned the knob, and felt her apprehension turn to disappointment at the emptiness of the space. There was just a bed, an end table, an armoire, and a round braided rug.

Grace shivered as she dropped her bag on the floor and sat on the end of the bed. She was exhausted after the long drive, the unnerving experience outside, and her sister's frigid welcoming. Tears welled up in her eyes as the realization that she'd missed seeing her mother for the last time sank in.

She took in the room, remembering where some of her things used to be. She had a magnificent wooden armoire in the far corner that held all her dresses and jackets. By the window, there was a little table and chairs that held pretend tea parties; that made her smile, remembering how huge her dad looked when he sat down with her once, so long ago.

In the middle of the room, on a large blue rug, there once sat her favorite toy, an antique wooden dollhouse. It was a replica of Craigrook House made by one of Grace's great-great uncles and had been passed down in the family for years. It was made entirely of wood and had windows and doors that opened and closed. The paint colors, wallpapers, and furnishings all closely mirrored the real Craigrook.

The dolls were all handmade as well, porcelain and cloth, and quite fragile. Grace always played with great care. They were all dressed in grand Victorian gowns and suits, right down to their crinolines and lacy pantaloons.

Grace recalled one time specifically when Morvin sat down on the floor beside her while she played with them.

"Hi, Gracey. Guess what? Mother's gone out for the *whole* day," she extended the word whole as she said it. "That means it's just you and me...all alone."

Grace had tried to ignore her and continued playing, but she was afraid of what being alone with Morvin might entail. Usually, it wasn't favorable for Grace.

"Can I play too?" asked Morvin.

"Uh, okay," answered Grace.

For a little while, it had been okay. Morvin was using the mommy doll and just walking it up and down the floors. Grace was playing with the daddy doll in the little study. Morvin brought the mommy downstairs, and she started making them kiss and hug. At first, Grace giggled, she was only five and seeing Mommy and Daddy kiss was funny. But then Morvin began making them do gross things. She was putting the daddy's hands under mommy's dress and making gross noises.

"Stop it, Morvin. I don't like it," Grace said.

Morvin continued and started making the daddy be mean to the mommy, hitting her and throwing her around.

Grace got up to leave. "Sit down!" Morvin demanded. "I'm in charge of you today, and I demand that you stay put, or I'll tell Mother that you wouldn't listen to me."

Grace sat down again and watched Morvin grab the little girl doll. Morvin tried to sound like a baby, "Ooh, Mommy! What is Daddy doing to you?" Then in a gruff daddy's voice, "Shut up, stupid child. How dare you barge in here!" She took the child doll and put it in the little closet at the back of one of the large bedrooms. "You'll stay in here until you've learned your lesson," she said, still using the daddy's voice.

"Daddy's aren't mean like that, Morvin," Grace said and went to take the girl out of the closet.

"Leave it!" yelled Morvin. "That little girl was bad, and she has to stay in that closet forever!"

"No!" Grace was getting upset. "Please go away, and let me play."

"You know what? You're a bad little girl too, arguing with me all day. I think you should go into the closet."

"No, Morvin. I don't want to. You can play, do whatever you want. Here." She tried to hand over the mommy doll, but Morvin batted it out of her hand. It flew to the other side of the room and hit the wall.

Grace started wailing. Morvin forced her to stand by pulling her shirt and forcefully led her into the room next door. She opened up the closet and pushed Grace to the floor. She slammed the door shut and left Grace crying in the darkness.

"Please, Morvin, I'm scared in here. It's too dark."

Grace could hear Morvin moving something heavy across the floor. She was moving something in front of the door. Grace tried to push the door open, but it wouldn't budge.

"You did this to yourself, you whiny little brat. Now you can stay in there forever like your stupid little doll. I'll tell Mother that I couldn't find you, and you'll die in there, all alone, forever."

Grace was still crying hard. She heard Morvin walk away.

"Oh, and by the way, I think I saw a rat in there."

Grace started to scream and banged on the door, pleading for Morvin to let her out. It was completely black in the cramped space, and her young imagination created horrors in the darkness. She could feel something scamper across her bare legs. Grace screamed and yelled for so long she began to lose her voice. Exhaustion finally took hold, and she fell asleep in the closet.

Just before their mother got home, Morvin opened the door and nudged Grace awake with her foot. "Get up, lazybones," she sang in a delighted voice. "Mother will be home soon, and if you're lucky, I won't tell her the disgusting things you did with your dolls."

Grace remembered being too tired to argue and also relieved to be out of her dark prison. It hurt to relive the awful experiences she endured as a child; it was all so unfair and unnecessary. At the time, though, Grace thought she deserved it all. Now she knew it was Morvin's vile manipulation of her young, naive mind.

Where was the dollhouse now? It had to be somewhere in the house. After all, it was an heirloom.

Grace changed into some warm pajamas and climbed beneath the crisp, cold sheets. She lay for some time, listening to the creaks of the old place. Same old creaks. Same old memories.

Same old Morvin.

CHAPTER TEN

"BUT THAT CAN'T be!" shouted Morvin.

Grace was just as shocked to discover that the entire estate and the fifty million dollar inheritance was to be hers alone. It didn't make any sense.

Jackson Humbly looked up at Morvin over his reading glasses. *Here we go,* he thought grimly. Morvin was standing now. "I'm afraid those were your mother's wishes, Ms. Knowles. The document is quite clear."

In a few hours, Jackson Humbly would be well on his way to the lake. He and his wife of forty years spent most of the spring and summer months at their cabin. This visit would be their last of the year; time to close it up already for another winter. The Calhoun reading was his last meeting of the day, and he couldn't wait for it to end.

"Calhoun! My name is Calhoun. How can this be?

It's an utter outrage. Let me see that." Morvin approached the desk and physically bumped Humbly to the side. "When was this changed?" she asked, scanning through the legal papers.

"Morvin really, compose yourself. We'll figure this all out. It's not Mr. Humbly's fault." Grace, embarrassed, tried to reason with her hostile sister.

She swallowed hard and shrank back as Morvin's gaze turned slowly toward her. Morvin's eyes narrowed into slits, filled with seething hatred; a look Grace remembered all too well. Feelings of insignificance and worthlessness overcame her, and she looked down. She learned very early on in life to never disagree or argue with Morvin.

"Just what the hell do you know?" Morvin said through her teeth. "You show up here and think you're going to take over? Don't you even think for a second this money is yours." She turned again to Jackson. "I asked you a question. When did Mother do this?"

Morvin was towering over the stout, balding lawyer. "Excuse me," he said sternly and moved Morvin aside as he stood up. He took the file from her and walked to the tall filing cabinet to the side of his desk. He opened a drawer and began rifling through documents. "She called a few months ago and made arrangements to meet. I assure you she was of sound mind, and it is my job as a loyal, trusted friend and legal representative of your family, to see that her final wishes are carried out."

Jackson Humbly had been the family lawyer and friend of their father as far back as Grace could remember. He was a pleasant man, quiet, with an honest face. He extracted another file and walked to the front of his desk.

"Now, I just need a signature here from both of you." He looked over his glasses at Grace.

"I'm not signing anything," Morvin said. "Grace doesn't deserve one damn penny."

"Yeah," voiced a young man with fiery red hair. He joined Morvin beside the desk. "She doesn't deserve nothin'. This is all wrong, man." He pointed a finger in Grace's direction. "Who the hell do you think you are?" Grace assumed this must be Morvin's son, Keaton. He was skinny, quite tall, dressed in a rock concert t-shirt and black jeans. He had striking blue eyes like Grace's father's, but the similarities stopped there. You could tell there wasn't much intelligence; he had a wild, deviant look to him.

"Please," said Grace, "I'm not here to do anything but bury my mother. This is not my doing." Grace never wanted any of her family's money. Even if she lost her bookstore, she would never accept help from the two people that had treated her so horribly. Why would their mother do this? Never a card or a letter but here's the family fortune? "Mr. Humbly, is there anything in there explaining this, or could there be a mistake?"

"You're damned right this is a mistake," Morvin fumed. She banged her fist on the desk. "Jackson, you fix this. Fix this immediately!" Spittle flew from Morvin's mouth as she enunciated every consonant through her teeth. She glared over at Grace. "You stay the hell out of this. This will not be yours."

Memories of all the times her sister talked down to her, treated her this way, came rushing back to Grace.

Morvin continued, "You don't deserve a dime, but,

just like always, everything falls into your stupid little lap. Well, not this bloody time."

"Morvin, please," Grace tried to reason. "If you calm down we'll figure all this out, I'm sure. Screaming and yelling will get us nowhere. My goodness, what a spectacle you're making." She took a deep breath and tried to stop herself from shaking.

Keaton uttered a grumbling comment. Morvin's face tightened, shocked by Grace's sudden and unfamiliar backbone.

"Grace is right, Morvin," Humbly said, as he pulled at his collar. "Let's all just calm down and take our seats." He checked his watch and sighed. He knew this was going to happen. Why was this always the way? The last appointment never failed to be the longest. He motioned to a chair, looking at Morvin.

Morvin jutted out her jaw and straightened her dress. Setting her shoulders, she addressed the lawyer directly. "I'm leaving this with you, Humbly, but know this…I will not let this happen, and if you can't set it right, I'll find someone who will. You can bet your damned life on that." She gave Grace another death glare as she exited the room. Keaton did the same as he followed her and slammed the door behind them.

"Mr. Humbly, I apologize for my sister's behavior." Grace stood and approached the desk. She picked up a pen and signed where Jackson was pointing. "Honestly, though, it is very odd. Why would my mother leave everything to me? She hasn't spoken to me once in all these years."

"All I can tell you is that she was one sad woman when I went to see her." Humbly straightened out the papers, tapping them together on his desk. "She was quite frail and weak too. I did run her through the usual questions to check that she knew what she was doing, and she did, no doubt about it. I asked her why she was she wanted the will changed, but she wouldn't elaborate. She just said that you would understand eventually." He sat back down behind his desk, his large belly pressed against the drawer handle. "I will say this though, Grace, she was very nervous the whole time I was there. I believe she was frightened of something. Now that I see Morvin's temper, I can understand why."

CHAPTER ELEVEN

G RACE WOKE WITH a start. For a second she didn't know where she was. Then the fog cleared and her surroundings became familiar once again. She didn't like sleeping in her old room. It was once a bright, yellow, cheery space but as Grace grew older, it became just another place of torment and stress.

Grace got up and went to one of the tall, skinny windows to draw the heavy curtains, with the hope that some daylight might lift the room's dismal atmosphere. No such luck. It was raining again. On days like this, there was never any sense of morning or afternoon, it always looked like six or seven in the evening, like the day couldn't wait to end.

There was no trace in the room that a child ever lived here at all. All of Grace's trinkets and toys were gone, even the numbered teddy bear picture her grandmother had bought for her fifth birthday was missing, only the square gray memory of it remained on the wall. The bed was the same, but with a different coverlet, the wallpaper was also the same, but the yellow swirls and bright orange blossoms were faded and dull, adding to the sense of sorrow and gloom. A perfect room for dealing with the grief of losing her mother, Grace thought. She couldn't shake the despair of not making peace or saying goodbye.

After Grace dressed, she decided to tour the old house and get an idea of what it would take to get it ready for sale, if that was the plan. Morvin certainly didn't need all this immense space and twelve plus rooms. It was evident that she wasn't able to keep up with the general maintenance, never mind the hours and hours of dusting and cleaning it required. With no servants in service any longer and Morvin the only one taking care of the grounds, the once enchanting estate was dilapidated.

Grace made her way down the main stairs to the foyer. How many times had she run her hands down the oak banister as she jumped down two or three stairs at a time? She recalled sitting on the carpeted steps, peeking through the wrought iron balusters with their unique Scottish thistle design, waiting for her father to walk through the door—most of the time in vain, for he was a busy man with his political work during the week and his favorite fly-fishing hobby almost every weekend.

The dark oak foyer gave entrance to the sitting room on the right, Father's library to the left, and the kitchen straight down the back hall.

"Okay, Grace, tea before all else," she said to herself.

The kitchen in Craigrook House was smaller than

one would expect in such a grand mansion. It was homey and comfortable, not cold or sterile, like many other period houses. She filled the kettle with water and lit the gas. She still knew where everything was. The tea bags, spoons, and sugar were all in the same spots. While her tea steeped, Grace gazed out the kitchen window at the grounds beyond. She had visions of herself as a girl running through the tall field grass, Morvin chasing her, her chasing Morvin. A grin spread on her face but faded as her memories continued. She could now see Morvin tripping her and then busting a gut as Grace cried, holding her scraped and bloody knee.

Grace was brought back to the present by the whistling kettle. She prepared her cup and took it with her back to the foyer, following the threadbare, hand-painted floor cloth into the large, oak-paneled sitting room.

It was like stepping back in time. All the same furniture in all the same places. Why had they kept this room like a mausoleum but threw out everything from Grace's room?

She walked over to the wood-burning fireplace, ran her fingers along the Adam-style mantel. She tried to bring forth memories of a warm fire burning and crackling, her family gathered together for Christmas morning or someone's birthday celebration. Some pleasant memories were there, but they never ended well, not for her; most of them marred by Morvin's incessant taunting or pinching or hurtful comments.

Grace took in the heaviness of the room. The dark, plush fabrics and sunless, shadowy corners. It was painful to be back here. The faster she got the arrangements made, and the will settled, the faster she could put this behind her once more.

Grace heard someone busying themselves with dishes in the kitchen. She wasn't ready to deal with Morvin yet this morning, so she dashed across the grand foyer to her father's library, where there were some good memories.

She entered the spacious study slowly, giving each recollection a chance to be savored. The handsome den housed an expansive library of all genres. Gooseflesh prickled Grace's arm as she stood in the center of her father's most treasured space that just happened to be Grace's favorite room in the house as well. Her love of books, literature, and ancient architecture began right here.

Grace inhaled deeply through her nose and reveled in the smell of must, dust and ancient ink, pulp and paper. She smiled as she took in the familiar sights and aromas she still cherished. She ran her hand along the deep brown, walnut siding and felt a wave of nostalgia when she saw the rose-colored gas lamps on each corner of her father's magnificent mahogany and oak pedestal desk. The windows, draped in heavy, coffee-colored, velvet curtains, stretched from floor to ceiling. Grace pushed one aside, amazed at the weight of it and repelled by the thick cloud of dust it emitted. She coughed into her hand and moved toward the massive book collection on three shelved walls.

Her father took immense pride in his books, Grace remembered. He'd had a deep love of reading and instilled in Grace respect for the written word at a young age.

Grace's father had disappeared suddenly while on one of his weekend fishing trips when she was only fourteen. He just never came home again. Speculation was that he had fallen into a rapidly flowing river and drowned. He was seen by a fellow fisherman early that morning. They had waved at each other, and went on their way and that was the last time anyone saw him.

After that, Grace's mother became miserable and gave up on life. Morvin's abusive behavior toward Grace worsened, and as Grace got older, she did begin to fight back somewhat, but so many years of torment had severely damaged her self-esteem. The verbal abuse continued to beat Grace down until she finally went away to boarding school.

Thick dust and cobwebs shrouded the books and shelves. When was the last time anyone visited this room or held one of the books? It was sad really that no one cared about all the hidden gems in this vast storehouse of knowledge and literature. As Grace made her way from one wall to the other, she noticed something out of place. In all this dust and *oose*, one book was curiously dust-free. Someone had looked at this one recently. She picked it off the shelf. *Botanical Poisons.* Grace flipped through some pages as she took a seat behind the desk. One was slightly dog-eared. It was a section about the water hemlock plant.

"I've made some eggs, seeing as you're still here," announced a deep, loud voice rather abruptly from the doorway. It was Morvin. "Why are you snooping about in this graveyard?"

"Oh my goodness, Morvin," Grace gasped and covered the book with her hand. "You gave me a fright. I'm just reminiscing a little. I've missed the old house." She stood and moved to the front of the desk. "I used to love sitting behind this desk pretending to be important like Father."

"Pretending is right," Morvin chided. "You better come get your breakfast before the eggs get cold. I abhor food waste above all else." Morvin waited in the doorway for Grace to follow.

"I'll be right there. I'm just a little teary-eyed. Give me two seconds?"

As soon as Morvin harrumphed and left, Grace whipped out her cell phone and quickly took a snap of the picture and article. She had the distinct feeling the book might mysteriously 'disappear' after she replaced it.

CHAPTER TWELVE

COLD, RUBBERY EGGS on soggy, butter-drenched toast; breakfast of champions. Grace knew she shouldn't complain, Morvin did make it for her. She scraped most of the breakfast into the garbage and noticed a gold shine reflecting off the steel lid. Is that? No, it couldn't be...sun!

Back home, Grace was a regular morning runner and rarely missed a day. Thinking she'd better take advantage of the rare break in the weather, she bounded upstairs and laced up her old sneakers. Grace whipped her hair into a ponytail and grabbed her cell phone off the nightstand.

Maybe a run would help her make sense of all this madness with the will. She had to admit, the money would solve a lot of problems and allow her to keep her bookstore but would also go against her principles. And there was still the question of why? Why had her mother left the inheritance to her and not Morvin, the daughter who looked after her?

She jogged down the country road that ran alongside the thousand-acre estate and soon felt her mood brighten with every step. She inhaled deeply, devouring the earthy, herb-like scent of the heather-clad moors, something she had sorely missed since moving away from Scotland.

The tremendous property boasted a remarkable diversity of landscape, from enchanting woodland to pretty lochs with jumping sea and brown trout and, in the distance, gentle contours amongst the rolling hills and farmland. Grace spotted a red grouse in a heather field and heard its distinct call that sounded like, "Goway, goway, goway."

"Don't worry," Grace said as she passed. "I won't bother you." She remembered when she was a little girl, her father enjoying grouse shoots at this time of year.

Grace found her rhythm, the pounding of her shoes on the road beating in sync with her breath. When she entered this point in her run, she felt she could go on forever. It was exhilarating. She crested a hill and took in the breathtaking scenery of Blackmore River. If she was lucky, she might come across a roe deer or a buck along the edge of the water.

She found herself thinking again of her father, who loved to fly-fish here. He'd once told her of a mythical creature called a Kelpie that was said to haunt Scotland's lochs and lonely rivers. A Kelpie, he explained, was a supernatural water-horse that would appear to its victims, mostly children, as a lost dark gray or white pony.

"Once you're on its back," he regaled, "you can't get

off, you're trapped…and then the Kelpie will drag you into the river and eat you!" She remembered him grabbing her then and the feel of his tickly beard as he pretended to gobble her up. She smiled and rounded a bend in the road that led away from the water toward a lush, green glen.

At the top of another small hill, she saw a man sitting to the side of the road. He was rubbing his leg.

"Everything okay?" she asked as she approached.

"Bloody leg cramp," he answered, wincing.

Grace looked at his rock hard calf muscle, which was bulging angrily. Being a runner herself, she knew that pain all too well.

"You have to get up and walk on it," she advised.

"Ach, I know, but it hurts." He rolled the 'r' in hurts, and she immediately felt a fondness for his Scottish accent, so much like her father's.

These days, Grace sounded more English than Scottish, having spent so many years there, away from her roots. Morvin had also lost a lot of her broad Scottish accent, but only because she thought the English sounded posher. She had always refused to use any Scottish slang; she had no pride in her heritage.

"Glaswegian?" Grace asked.

"Aye. Is it that obvious? Gee us a hand, will ye' lass?" he asked. He put one hand on a rustic, drystone fence for support, and Grace took the other.

She helped the handsome Scot to his feet. He cringed and moaned as he tried to put weight on his leg.

"My dad was from Pollock," said Grace, as she bent down for a better look at his leg. "Wow, it's incredibly stiff. I'll try rubbing it a bit. Maybe I can soften it for you."

The man grinned mischievously down at her. "I highly doubt that."

Grace flushed a bright red, and she stood back up, averting his eyes—his gorgeous sky-blue eyes.

"Excuse me. That was rude. I just could'na help myself." He put out his hand. "I'm Cameron. Cameron Elliot."

Grace immediately recognized the name. "The author, Cameron Elliot?" She had read one of his novels, spy thrillers. Not her preferred genre, but she remembered enjoying it.

"Yes, you've read me?" he asked.

"I have. You're quite good." Grace smiled.

"Gee, thanks," he smiled back, and Grace melted a bit. "My leg feels a bit better. Care to jog wi' me for a stretch? In case I need help again?" He moved some hair out of his eyes and flicked it back with a jerk of his head. A move she couldn't help but think was damned sexy.

They jogged slowly, side by side, him with a slight limp that soon disappeared. Their chatting continued as they passed waves of rugged green farmland and vast sheep farms, a common sight in this area of the Edinburgh countryside.

Grace learned he was renting the old Gittens' cottage beside her family's estate, trying to finish his latest novel. She explained that she was visiting temporarily, dealing with family matters.

"Sounds like grrr-eat fun," he said. There was that sexy rolling 'r' again.

"Oh yeah, it's a regular laugh riot." Grace saw that the road leading to her property was approaching on her right.

She increased her speed and left his side, moving past him. Just as she was about to make her exit, she turned coolly and jogged backward.

"Well, this is me," she said. "Maybe we'll run into each other again sometime, and I can help you with another hard muscle." She couldn't believe how her comment had come out, how it must have sounded to him. She was so embarrassed she nearly tripped over her own feet but caught herself just in time. Without looking back at him, she waved and sprinted up the driveway.

"Real smooth, Gracey," she muttered to herself, feeling like an idiot. She did catch him grinning, though, before she darted away, and found that she couldn't help but smile a little herself.

CHAPTER THIRTEEN

T HE GROAN AND clang of the old pipes echoed through the house as Grace cranked on the hot water for her shower. The small bathroom on the second floor had the most updated fixtures; unfortunately, it was at the opposite end of the mansion.

She went to the mirror as she waited for hot water to reach the pipes and frowned at her reflection. The giant bags under her eyes were a testament to her restless sleep. Steam finally began to fog the mirror, but just as she was ready to step under the hot spray, she heard the shrill of the telephone. She paused for a second or two, debated ignoring it, but what if it was about the will. Grace sighed, wrapped herself in a towel, and ran downstairs to the kitchen.

"Hello?" said Grace, into the heavy handset of the yellow rotary phone, circa 1978.

"Is this the Calhoun/Bircham residence?"

"Yes, it is. Grace Calhoun speaking."

"This is Riggart County Hospital. May I speak with Margaret Calhoun, please?"

"I'm sorry, she recently passed away." Grace realized that was the first time she had said those words out loud. It was real. "I'm her daughter, maybe I can help?"

The woman on the other side said with authority, "Well, the Calhoun's are listed as the only next of kin, so yes, that will do. I'm sorry to inform you that Ms. Lena Bircham has been admitted to our facility and is currently under observation in the intensive care ward." She had a very thick Scottish brogue.

"Oh, no! Aunt Lena?" Lena Bircham was Grace's mother's younger sister. She hadn't seen her since she left for university in England. They had been quite close once, long ago. A memory of the time her aunt took little Grace shopping at the large mall in Edinburgh flashed through her mind. Grace stood up a little straighter. "What happened?"

"It seems she has possibly suffered a stroke or an aneurism. The doctor in charge is currently confirming the diagnosis."

Grace turned her head toward the front door as the doorbell chimed.

"My goodness. Is she going to be okay? Can I see her?" Grace asked, trying to ignore the second ringing of the visitor at the door.

"At present, it's at the doctor's discretion. She is somewhat agitated, though, which is quite common for stroke victims. So, if and when she's cleared for visitation, you'll have to keep it short and try your best not to distress the patient."

"I'll be there within the hour." She wrote down the ward number and hung up the phone, then tightened the knot in her towel and went to answer the door.

"What now?" she muttered as she walked to the foyer. "Yes?" Grace asked, opening the door just enough for her head to poke out.

"Grace Calhoun?" asked a very tall, well-dressed gentleman.

"Yes, that's me."

He smirked and checked out Grace's bare shoulder as he handed her an official-looking letter.

"What's this?" Grace asked.

"My name is Piers Thornhill. I've been solicited to represent Ms. Morvin Knowles to contest the will of one Margaret Fleming Bircham Calhoun." He didn't look Grace in the eye even once as he spoke. His face was thin but handsome, and his brown, slick hair had a perfect wave at the front, giving him a suave, debonair quality.

"What? There has to be some mistake." Grace exclaimed. "I told my sister I would ensure that we'd sort all this out fairly. I don't even want the money. This is ridiculous." She let the door open fully as she slammed the letter into her thigh.

He put his back to her and began walking away, apparently done with the conversation.

"Just a damned minute, sir!" Grace demanded to his back, forgetting that she was only wearing a towel.

He waved a hand in the air without looking back. "It's all in the letter, Miss Calhoun. I'll be in touch."

"But—" Grace said, but he was already getting into his silver BMW. She raised her arms, exasperated, but exasperation turned to horror as she felt her towel slacken and fall to the pavement. Appalled, Grace retrieved it, dropping the letter in the process. A sudden gust of wind caught the damn thing and carried it down the steps. She went after it and nearly tripped over her towel, losing it once again. Panicked, Grace grabbed the towel and draped it around her loosely with her right arm. However, she was not able to cover herself entirely as her arm was too weak, and her hand not physically able to grasp fully. Meanwhile, the letter was still gaily flapping away from her, down the driveway, staying just out of her left hand's reach.

Mr. Thornhill seemed to be thoroughly enjoying the spectacle by the look on his grinning face as he drove past her. He exited the driveway as slowly as possible so as not to miss a second of the show.

Finally, Grace caught up with the letter as the wind died, and it came to rest on the grass beside the drive. Keeping her head down, she put the letter snugly between her knees as she readjusted the slippery damned towel and secured it tightly once more. Grace ran to the steps, feeling the sting of a few sharp rocks on her bare feet. She couldn't get back to the house fast enough. As she closed the door, she saw the bumper of his car turn the corner of the driveway. She leaned on the inside of the door and put a hand to her mouth.

"Did that really just happen?" She was exhausted and extremely embarrassed. "Grace, you are one Class A klutz...oh my bloody God."

She shook her head and opened the letter as she walked back upstairs to the bathroom. The legal jargon was impossible to understand. Grace rubbed her forehead aggressively, feeling a massive headache coming on.

CHAPTER FOURTEEN

THE NOISE AND commotion in the intensive care unit blasted Grace as she entered the ward. The hectic activity of nurses and doctors, the phones ringing, the unsettling relentless call of various machines clamoring for attention—it was all an unpleasant assault on the ears.

Grace made her way to the nurse's station. She waited a few minutes for one of the nurses to acknowledge her presence. She wondered if they were too busy to notice or if they were ignoring her.

Finally, Grace said, "Excuse me." When no one looked up from their task, she knew it was the latter. Who could blame them? They looked short-staffed and overworked. "Sorry to bother you. Could you direct me to Lena Bircham's room?"

A weary face looked up at her and let out a long and

audible sigh. "Just a minute." She said a few monotone words to another nurse behind her and then joined Grace in front of the high circular desk. She was middle-aged and quite heavy and walked with a pronounced limp. Her whole body veered to one side with every labored step. She explained, without emotion, that Lena had been in and out of consciousness but was alert at the last vitals check.

"She is not able to speak at present, which is common in stroke victims, but she is trying to form words, so we're optimistic that speech may return." The nurse lumbered on as she spoke, stopping every so often to check a chart, spout off an order, or pick up a stray object and replace it. Grace had to listen closely as the woman was speaking face forward, not really to Grace at all. "Keep in mind there may be some permanent brain damage and loss of use of some parts of her body. We're not sure at this point the extent of the damage. Try to keep her calm, and please have a positive attitude when you see her." She stopped abruptly at the entrance to Lena's room, turned to Grace, and looked her directly in the eye. "Your visit will have to be short as we're still running tests."

Grace assured the nurse that she understood and entered the room. The door closed behind her, causing a noticeable decibel difference that was immediate and very welcome.

Aunt Lena had a private room that contained only a bed, one chair, and a metal nightstand. The pale blue walls added to the sterile coolness of the place.

Aunt Lena was lying very still with her eyes closed, and for a second, Grace thought the worst. As she got closer, though, she could hear a faint gurgling and saw that

Lena's chest was falling and rising lightly. She had drool running down one lip, and her skin was pallid and waxen.

Grace pulled up a chair and cringed when the metal legs screeched across the linoleum floor, which, in the tomb-like, empty room, echoed sharply.

"Hi, Auntie Lena," Grace whispered, as she sat down, keeping her voice soft.

Lena's eyelids flickered a few times then opened. Her red eyeballs turned in Grace's direction slowly and then widened as in shock or surprise. Lena began grunting through throaty gasps for breath. She coughed as she tried to speak, her grunting getting louder, her expression anguished and upset.

"Aunt Lena, calm down. You're going to be okay. I'm here. Please...try to rest." Grace was shocked at her aunt's apparent confusion and anxiety as Lena continued to become more and more distressed. Lena reached an arm out to Grace, all the while moaning and seemingly trying to convey something. She grabbed Grace's hand with surprising strength and looked pleadingly into Grace's eyes.

"Maaaaa, Maaaaarrrr," Lena moaned.

Grace assumed she was trying to say Margaret, her mother's name. "Yes, Auntie, I know. I'm sorry about Mum. But she's not suffering now. It's okay."

"Puuu, puuugh," she coughed and wheezed.

"You must try and relax, Aunt Lena. Please. You're scaring me."

Lena would not stop. She grabbed at Grace's hand and arm, pulling her closer to Lena's face and bulging eyes.

"Puuuuuuuuuu! Puuuuuuuu!" She dug her nails into Grace's skin, strong enough to draw blood.

A different nurse came charging through the door holding a syringe. "I'm afraid you'll have to leave."

"But I think she's trying to tell me something."

"It's common for stroke victims to be disoriented, confused, and scared." The burly nurse barged in between Grace and her aunt. "We'll give her something to help her rest now, but you'll have to go." She pointed at the door.

Grace got up slowly, not wanting to leave her aunt in such a state. Lena's hoarse gurgling got louder as Grace turned toward the door, her hand grasping at the air as if trying to pull Grace back to her.

"I've got to leave now, Auntie. I'm so sorry. I'll come back soon. You need to rest to get better. You'll be okay." Grace began tearing up, distraught at the sight of her poor old aunt in such a horrific state. She left the room, still able to hear her aunt's cries, and hurried out of the ward. She couldn't get out of the hospital fast enough, on the absolute verge of breaking down.

An elderly man at the entrance tried to stop her, to ask her something. Grace rushed past, trying not to make eye contact with anyone, fighting back an onslaught of emotion.

She raced through the parking lot, trying to see through her watery vision, to where she parked the damn car. At last, there it was in the far corner. Grace ran, fumbling with her keys as she went.

In the privacy of her car, she could release the bone in her throat, finally let the tears flow. She'd already lost her mother, now her aunt lay in the hospital, devastated by a stroke, and to top it all off, she still had to deal with her horrible sister. It was almost too much to bear.

CHAPTER FIFTEEN

GRACE WAS THANKFUL she had decided on her wool jacket and heavy scarf as she made her way through the grounds outside the mansion. It wasn't raining yet, but it was a typical Scottish morning in September, with a nip in the air and a mist on the ground.

Something Morvin said the night before had Grace wanting to take a closer look around the estate. She had barely batted an eye when Grace told her about their aunt being in the hospital. "She was old...things happen." She had said it so flippantly. And, Grace noticed, how she talked of Lena in the past tense.

"But isn't it strange that Mother just died of a heart attack, and now Aunt Lena seems to have had a stroke?" Grace asked.

Morvin again replied in the most uncaring manner,

"They didn't look after themselves, had no stimulating outlet. I've got my beautiful garden. That's my haven. It holds all my answers. It's all I need." She had this sinister, faraway look as she spoke. "Come to think of it," Morvin continued, but now her sneering gaze landed on Grace, "neither do you. Maybe you should be careful about your health too."

Grace shivered as she thought about their conversation, the way Morvin was acting.

She descended the back stairs and walked to the large patio. If you headed back from there, you'd end up at the pool area; left would take you to the back yard and forest beyond and, finally, heading right, where Grace was going, patchy moss-carpeted paths wound through once prided rose bushes, rhododendrons and such. Beyond that was Morvin's private garden.

She wondered if Morvin still fanatically tended her cherished plot of ground. Grace, nor anyone else, was ever allowed in there. Morvin forbade it. She remembered seeking it out a time or two as a curious little girl. The first few times she'd gotten away with, it but the last time, Morvin caught her, the hell she endured for that mistake was not worth the risk, and she never ventured to Morvin's sacred garden again.

She was five years old at the time, making Morvin around eighteen or so. It was summer, one of the warmest days that year. Grace remembered because she had been wearing her favorite sailor bathing suit with a little pleated skirt sewn into the waist. She knew she was not supposed to be in the garden, but it was so magical. Grace liked to imagine fairies or sprites dancing about among the many colorful flowers and whimsical garden ornaments.

"Looking for something?" Grace turned around quickly, startled by Morvin's deep voice.

"Fairies," Grace replied. "I think there are fairies in your garden." Maybe Morvin wouldn't be angry if she thought fairies were living here too. Perhaps she'd help Grace look for them.

"Hahaha…what a little fool you are." Morvin walked toward her quickly. "Get out!"

Grace backed up, made a move to the gate, trying to brush past her much bigger, older sister. Morvin grabbed Grace's right arm and yanked it hard, swirling Grace around to face her.

"What's that? What have you got in your greasy little mitt?" She snatched a pretty bluebell from Grace's grasp. "Killing things now? How dare you come in here, where you know you're forbidden, and steal one of my flowers?" Morvin pushed Grace in the chest, and she fell backwards, her rump landing on a sharp-edged rock. "Get out, I said!"

"I'm trying," Grace started to cry as she stood up, rubbing her sore bottom. "I'm sorry."

Morvin mimicked her, "I'm sorry. What a loser you are. Get out!" Morvin was yelling now. "I don't want you here. No one wants you here. Why don't you just run away? Go to the gimp hospital and be with other gimps. You don't belong here." Morvin grabbed the now crushed flower from Grace's small hand. "Oh, here, wait. You killed it so you may as well keep it. In fact," she grabbed Grace painfully by the wrist, "eat it."

"What?" said Grace, wiping the tears from her face.

"Deaf, you little wimp? I said, eat it." Morvin pressed the blue flower against Grace's lips, using her sharp nails to pry them open. Grace tried to hold them shut tight, but Morvin's nails were hurting her. She relented, and Morvin jammed the flower against her teeth and shoved it to the back of Grace's mouth. "Tell anyone, and you know what'll happen. Now *get out!*"

Thinking back on it brought tears again to Grace's eyes. She felt sorry for her younger self. It wasn't fair at all to have grown up in that environment. It took a long time for her to realize she didn't deserve it, and it wasn't her fault.

She continued to walk the grounds, saddened to see the vibrant, lush bushes and shrubs, once tended faithfully by greens keepers and landscapers, become such an intertwined mess of neglected, overgrown brush. She picked her way through the jungle by following a fairly well-worn path that was no doubt traveled frequently by Morvin on her way to her little piece of Eden. How could she, a lover of everything green, let the rest of the grounds fall to ruin like this?

Grace eventually came to the massive arbor, draped in wicked, gnarly, twisting vines that housed the entrance to Morvin's garden. The rusty, metal gate was barely visible. The hinge shrieked as she pushed it open. Entering the garden was like leaving one world behind and arriving in another.

It truly is beautiful, thought Grace, as she stood there and took in its splendor. Morvin did have an undeniable, extraordinary talent when it came to plants and flowers. Impatiens of all colors, still blooming but on their last burst of the season, bordered the lush green grass in a waving pattern. Beyond them were full, manicured rhododendrons, hydrangeas, and English lavender, which was their father's favorite. A sweet little iron table and chairs sat under a canopy of burgundy trumpet vines. The scene was enchanting.

Grace walked deeper into the botanical paradise. She heightened her thick scarf over her chin, denying the steel fingers of the icy breeze access to her bare skin. Following the narrow pebbled path flanked with meadowsweet, she came across a new addition—a frog pond, complete with water lilies and long green reeds along the edge.

Grace remembered reading that water hemlock grew near marshes and streams and took out her phone. She opened the pictures and the snap of the article she had taken in her father's library and scanned the foliage around the pond, comparing the image to a few unique looking plants.

Her eyes widened in disbelief. There it was. She reread the article: 'a poisonous plant that, when ingested, causes seizures, nausea, abdominal pain, and confusion. Death can occur in just a few hours by respiratory failure or ventricular fibrillation.'

Also known as...a heart attack.

Grace's ears twitched as she heard the gate open. She nearly tripped over a dew-covered rock but found her footing and scrambled behind the thick trunk of a large, prickly holly tree. She was shaking, crouched there, her eyes clenched shut, her heart hammering in her chest. She felt five years old again, terrified of being caught.

She listened for footsteps. A rustling came from the distance, maybe twenty feet away, across the pond for sure.

The sound continued, light and fluttery, getting closer. She chanced a peek around the tree and blew out a huge breath she hadn't realized she'd been holding. There, in the bordering ground cover by the pond, sat a plump brown hare, enjoying a morning nibble. It startled and took off like a shot when Grace emerged from her hiding place.

Deciding she'd seen enough, Grace took a quick picture of Morvin's coveted poisonous plant and left the garden. Morvin could quite possibly be up to something truly vile and unthinkable, even for her.

Grace was now on a mission to find out.

CHAPTER SIXTEEN

"MOTHER, CAN I get an advance on next week's allowance, plus just a little extra? Me and Gav need to up our tool inventory for this gardening gig." Keaton knew if he related anything to gardening or landscaping, his mother would be pleased.

Morvin looked up from her half-chopped green onions.

"Not a chance. You're already a week ahead in your allowance. You've got to learn to be more responsible with money, Keaton." She shook her head at him.

It seemed she was always shaking her head at him lately, just like Granny did. He had become so sick of hearing that selfish old bat always telling him how fortunate he was to be in this family and that he should go out and make his difference. What the hell did that mean anyway?

"Stop wasting your time on these games," Granny

would always say when he asked for anything. "You spend too much time on your behind in front of that screen, young man. There are men your age fighting wars and running countries while you sit there wasting your life." Oh man, he was getting one of his headaches just thinking about her nagging voice. She would look at him over her glasses and click her tongue at him, "Tsk, tsk, tsk." He stopped himself many times from blowing up at her or just winding up, and...but that would probably have landed him on the street. He wasn't that stupid. He always stole from her room later anyway...dumb old bat.

"By the way," said Morvin, "some man ringed for you this morning. And he was insulting and rude." Morvin wiped her hands on a kitchen towel and then folded her arms in front of her. "Are you in trouble again?"

Shit. The guy had his number now? Keaton rubbed at the back of his neck, remembering that gorilla-sized hand holding him by his shirt and shaking him around like a bag of sticks.

"Where's the money, eh? You little shit." The guy's head was the biggest Keaton had ever seen. He always wore the same gray hoodie with the sleeves pushed past his elbows, revealing massive tattooed forearms that would rival Popeye's.

He'd been following Keaton for weeks now. He saw him everywhere. At first, the guy just stood there, across the street from the arcade or casino. He'd stand there with a weird grin and point at Keaton, then rub his fingertips together in the money gesture. Keaton tried to ignore him and walk away in the opposite direction. Now Keaton was seeing him outside the house gates. Clearly, he knew where he lived and, apparently, also had his phone number. On Saturday, Keaton found a note on his car that read, 'Have exactly half of wat you owe by Friday, kid, or this is gonna get ugly.'

If his stupid-ass mother would hand over some cash, he knew he could double it at the casino and at least pay the guy something. He'd won a little at that hot chick's blackjack table lately. She was giving him the eye the other night. Maybe she'd go easy on him, let him win a few if he kept making moves on her. Maybe she'd let him get real lucky, later, after her shift.

Keaton ignored his mother's question and pressed on.

"But it's for work. I like working at the nursery, and with new tools, Charlie will give me more jobs."

He'd begun to reach that demanding octave, making Morvin slightly uneasy.

"Look, dear," she said, trying to soften him a bit, "you know you don't even have to worry about working. We'll have plenty of money when the will gets settled. Charlie only asks for your help when he needs a big strong boy around."

"I am *not* a boy! Just give me the money, Mum. I need it *now!*" He stomped forward on the last word causing Morvin to take a step back. Why did she always waste his time with her arguing? She always gave it to him in the end anyway. Couldn't we skip this bullshit for once?

"Keaton!" she yelled. She took a deep breath. "Calm down. What have you gotten yourself into this time? You've been gambling again, haven't you?" It wouldn't be the first time Keaton gambled and lost. Just last year, she'd had to ask her mother for money to pay off his credit cards. That was humiliating. Now, with all the money tied up in the will and possibly going to Grace, she might not be able to help him at all. What then? She couldn't bear the thought.

"And you're probably smoking marijuana too," she continued. "I want you to stop hanging around with that Matthew; he's nothing but a loser. You're better than that. You come from good blood, Keaton. What's wrong with you? When are you going to get it together?"

Even though he was a little slow at getting started, Morvin always believed he had greatness in him. As a young boy, he was so very bright. It was middle school when the problems began.

"Here we go," said Keaton. "I just told you what the fucking money's for. Is there something wrong with your hearing?" He moved closer, looming over her. "I hate when you think I'm always lying. Maybe I should take off, never see you again. How would that be?"

Morvin couldn't bear the thought of losing her son. He was all she had left in the world. Even Keaton's father had left them; everyone left them. Money was so tight right now but wouldn't be if there wasn't this issue with the will. Now she had to wait and fight for what was rightly theirs. And fight she would. Grace had always gotten everything she ever wanted, little princess. Not this time.

"Are you lying to me again, Keaton? You can talk to me, son." She went to move his red hair off his face, but he swatted her arm away.

"Yeah, okay, look. Someone's after me for money. And I'm fucking scared, Mum. So help me out here. Please."

He gave her the best sorrowful look he could muster to convince the stupid bitch to cough up.

"Well," Morvin stammered, "I guess I can manage a little extra right now." She lifted her purse from a kitchen chair, opened her wallet, and handed Keaton two twenty pound notes. Keaton snatched the money out of her hand and then grabbed her purse.

"I'll be having all of it," he growled. He took the remaining cash out of Morvin's wallet. "This is it? Is this all you have?" A lousy fifty wasn't going to be enough. Now he'd have to find another way to get money or 'Mr. Forearms' was going to lay some serious hurt on him. He took out Morvin's Visa and smashed her wallet on the counter, crushing her green onions beneath it

Without looking at her or saying another word, he turned and left the house, slamming the door behind him.

Morvin put her hand to her throat and closed her mouth, then turned and numbly went about cleaning up the mess on the counter.

He was fuming as he got behind the wheel of Morvin's car. He reached into his pocket for his keys...not there.

"Fucking bitch's got me all screwed up."

He ran back to the front door but turned when he felt eyes on him. Was that someone watching him? Keaton was terrified of the enormous guy following him. He scanned the driveway as he backed up the stairs. He missed the last step and went down hard on his bony ass.

"Awe, shit!" he cried out. "What was that?" he heard

a noise from the side hedge. Prickles of panic crept up the back of his neck as he got to his feet. Keaton took one last quick look over his shoulder and entered the house.

He checked the sitting room for his keys, then the kitchen. Maybe he left them upstairs. He scaled the large staircase two stairs at a time and stopped at the top.

Why was there music coming from his dead grandmother's room?

CHAPTER SEVENTEEN

*I*T CAN'T BE *right,* thought Grace, as she made her way through the large mansion to her mother's bedroom on the third floor. She was stunned after discovering the poisonous plant in Morvin's garden.

She carried a large empty box. If it looked like she was starting to pack up Mother's things, Morvin wouldn't suspect that she was snooping.

Grace stood in the middle of her mother's bedroom. Strange how the scent of her perfume still lingered, but the wearer, her mother, was gone. She remembered sitting at the brass vanity in the corner after an evening bath, her mother brushing her hair behind her.

She began putting items, one by one, into the box. Each one created in her mind a short movie about her past. Grace opened the top drawer of the vanity and riffled through some papers. There were some old pictures of her dad, herself, and Morvin, who wasn't smiling in any of them.

"What's this?" she asked no one in particular. Under the old photos was a little children's book that her mother used to read to her. Grace sat back in the vanity chair and smiled to herself. "*Racketty-Packetty House*," she said aloud, nodding. Her mother loved this book even more than Grace did.

She carefully opened the timeworn cover; the date on the inside read 1906, and it appeared to be a first edition. The little gem was bound in original blue cloth. The spine was worn, of course, but it was in pretty good shape. "You're not going in the box, little beauty." She put it to the side.

She walked over to her mother's nightstand and picked up a music box that Grace had given her for a Christmas gift many years ago. She wiped the dust off the top and lifted the heavy glass lid. *Lara's Theme* began to play in plucky little notes that made Grace's eyes fill with tears. The tune echoed hauntingly in the large bedroom. "You're a keeper too." She put it on the night table beside the book and let the song play as she continued with her task.

"Nice tunes."

Grace was startled and drew in a loud gasp. Keaton was standing leisurely in the doorway with a smirk on his pocked face. He entered the room and walked over to her.

"Hello, Keaton," said Grace. "I guess it's time we started packing some stuff away. Brings back a lot of memories, though."

Keaton approached her as she knelt beside the large

box. He was standing uncomfortably close, his belt buckle right in her face. Grace stood up and moved away from him, but he followed her closely.

"What do you want, Keaton? I'm busy here." Grace started feeling uneasy by his pressuring manner and strange expression. He backed her up against the wall. She put her hand against his chest to stop him, but he closed right in on her.

"You know what your problem is, Auntie Gracey? You're hard up. I think a little Keaton action will loosen you up just nicely." He fingered the buttons on her cardigan. "Let's have a look at what's under that tight little sweater of yours."

His yellow teeth were just inches from her eyes. He was taller than her, and although he was skinny, he looked sinewy and thug-tough. He put his hand on her breast as he continued to press her into the wall with his hardening body.

"Get the hell away from me!" Grace tried to push him off. He grabbed her left arm and raised it, pinning it to the wall, hurting her wrist. She couldn't fight him off with her frail right arm, a fact he was aware of, unfortunately.

"What ya' gonna do now, wounded sparrow? Come on. You want it. I know you do." He was breathing his putrid breath all over her neck, nearly making her gag. He started gyrating hard against her body. He laughed. He was enjoying himself.

"I said, let me go!" Grace slammed her heel onto his toes, causing him to keel forward, releasing her arm in the process. She grabbed a handful of his greasy hair and drove his face into her knee and then pushed him away. He fell to the ground, cursing and holding his nose.

"You stupid bitch. Look what you did to my nose. I think it's fucking broken!"

Grace was making her way to the doorway when Morvin appeared in front of her.

"What's going on?" she demanded.

"Your son just assaulted me!" Grace was out of breath. "He came in here and put his hands on me, and he pinned me against the wall." She looked at Keaton. "You're a sick bastard! There's something wrong with you."

"Yeah, right. Like I would want an old whore like you." He got to his feet. "Lucky thing I forgot my keys, Mum. I was on my way out again but stopped and came in here because I heard Granny's music box playing, and she started yelling at me to get out. She punched me in the face because I wouldn't leave her alone to snoop in Granny's things."

"I'll have you up on charges if you ever touch my son again," Morvin said, pointing her finger at Grace. She helped Keaton out of the room to tend to him. "His nose better not be broken, or I'll have you arrested!"

Grace stood there, her mouth hanging open, not quite able to grasp what just happened. She shook her head in disgust and disbelief.

"He accosted ME!" she yelled at them as they walked away down the hall toward the bathroom. "Well," Grace said to herself, "you'd be proud of me, Devi. Those lessons were worth every damn penny."

She straightened her blouse and smoothed her disheveled hair off her face, then grabbed the little children's book and walked down the hall to her room, slamming the door behind her.

CHAPTER EIGHTEEN

"HOW DARE SHE!" fumed Morvin. Keaton's nose was fine, not broken, thank goodness, but he was hurt emotionally by that meddling bitch.

Morvin headed to her sanctuary. The one place where nothing could touch her, nothing could hurt her. As soon as she walked through the gate, she instantly felt better. She had always found peace with her plants. They didn't argue or even have an opinion. They were grateful for all they received, rewarding you with flowers, food, and beauty. They didn't try to outdo you, and they didn't judge or disappoint; they just were. And she adored them all.

Morvin knelt before one of the bordering plants. She began extracting some small weeds from her grand bed of Lavandula angustifolia, also known as English lavender. She tried to relax and enjoy her favorite pastime, but thoughts of Grace kept needling at her mind. Imagine accusing Keaton like that! Lies! Nothing but an absolute pain in the ass liar.

She's always been like this. Whining to everyone who would listen. 'Poor me, look at me, help me.' Sickening. Grace had everyone fooled, especially their father, always sitting on his knee, giggling away...disgusting.

Everything changed for Morvin after Grace had been born. They all fussed non-stop after her because of her gimpy arm. It was like Morvin didn't even exist to them anymore. She had tried to be kind to the little freak, but all that crying and all that demanding of everyone's attention was unbearable. And then that one night...that had been it for Morvin. All she did was stick out her foot, and it was an accident. Stupid Grace was always falling anyway, but father had lost it.

"That's the last straw!" he yelled. "I'm sending you away so that you can't hurt Grace any longer."

Mother begged him not to do it, pleaded with him. But his mind was made up, he'd said. He even said he was afraid she was going to kill Grace eventually! Imagine! Why couldn't he see that this was all Grace's fault and that she was playing everyone?

Morvin began pulling on a particularly stubborn weed. "Just who the hell does she think she is? Thinks every man wants her, always has." She was talking to herself out loud now, and her voice was steadily getting louder.

She felt her face warm as she gritted her teeth and pulled harder at the invading green culprit. "I will not let her get away with this. We were just fine here without her; meddling, self-righteous, stupid little bitch!" Morvin jabbed at the weed with her sharp fingernails, scratching and clawing at the dirt, sprays of spit flying out from her tight lips.

"Try and mess with me, you stupid, lame little whore. Just try, and I'll show you." Morvin grabbed a sharp, metal digging trowel and forcefully stabbed it into the earth, again, again and again. Over and over, she struck the small shovel into the ground, blindly destroying part of her precious lavender plant. Dirt and greenery flew out everywhere around her, her hair dampened around her face with sweat. Her fingers began to bleed with the force of the tiny rocks and roots in the soil.

With one final stabbing motion, she heard something snap. Morvin abruptly stopped her tirade and put the trowel down beside her. She looked at her hand and saw that her pinkie finger was facing the wrong way. She grabbed the finger with her other hand, pulled it, and twisted. Without so much as a whimper, she snapped it back into place.

She sat still for a while, exhausted and breathing heavily. Then she laid down on her back in the wet grass. She lay motionless, staring blankly up at the cloudy sky, oblivious even as a tiny spider ran across her face.

It started to rain after some time, causing Morvin to blink finally, and she brushed the wet strands of hair back from her face. She sat up and patted down the madly disturbed soil then took her tools to the garden shed. She calmly cleaned her trowel, smoothed out her dirty apron and skirt, and then paused in the middle of the room. She had that same blank look on her face as she stood there, unmoving.

A sudden wind picked up outside, blowing the large

fir tree by the window. A sharp branch scraped and banged against the glass, and still, Morvin stood there, unflinching, softly breathing. Finally, she turned her head and faced a dark corner.

"Shut up," she growled. She went about putting her tools away and then, once again, turned to the corner and a little louder this time said, "Shut up!" She stood as if waiting for a response. Then Morvin simply turned and left the shed, not bothering to close the door behind her. She sauntered back toward the house and entered through the back door, expressionless and calm.

CHAPTER NINETEEN

S HE SPENT THE whole night in her room, venturing out only to visit the small bathroom down the hall and, thankfully, at the opposite end of the house from Morvin's.

The hallway was cold, dark, and tomb quiet in the middle of the night. Grace used the light of her cell phone to see, which created long, creepy shadows all around her and brought back memories of being frightened just like this as a child. She loved the old house, but it could be downright eerie at night.

On the way back to her room, she felt that same terrifying feeling, as she always did all those years ago, of someone behind her in the long, ominous hall, and she ran the last few feet to her door. Almost twenty years later, and she could still practically feel the icy fingers of some angry spirit or ghoul about to touch her shoulder.

Once back under the safety of her covers, she felt rather silly at her behavior. However, it still took quite some time for her heart rate to return to normal and for the fine hairs on the back of her neck to settle.

She endured another fitful night and, at the predawn hour of 6:00 a.m., decided to give up on sleep and got out of bed. An early morning walk might do her some good, she thought. So she dressed warmly and went to grab her cell from the nightstand. It wasn't there. Didn't she just use it last night? Thinking it would probably turn up later, she slinked out the kitchen door, trying to avoid running into anyone.

Grace walked in the light rain, trying to organize her thoughts. So much was going on here. How could she make sense of it all? Morvin, a murderer? Maybe it was possible. Keaton, a rapist? Totally possible. Just the thought of him and their encounter made her shiver.

She wandered the grounds of the estate in deep thought, not paying much attention to where she was going. She eventually found herself down by the old swimming pool, long since emptied and no longer in use; now just a worn, empty, concrete space in the ground. This spot was where, finally, someone else saw Morvin's deep hatred for her.

She vividly remembered the horrible fright she got that day and could still taste the chlorine, feel it burning the back of her nose and throat as she frantically gasped for air. Old Wilson's weathered, worried face looked down at her while she vomited up a gallon of pool water. And Morvin's stone-faced expression watching her as she panicked, fighting to stay afloat in the deep pool. She remembered that terrifying feeling of there being no solid ground under her feet, sinking, panicking, dying.

Grace's mother had come running out of the house after Wilson had jumped in and saved her. The old groundskeeper began to explain that he had heard the splashing from over the hedge and had come to check it out. He declared how Grace had been thrashing and struggling, drowning in the deep end of the pool, while Morvin stood, watching from the shallows, doing nothing to save her.

"Why would you do that?" he asked Morvin angrily. "You know your sister can't swim with her bad arm. Why didn't you try and help her?"

"How dare you!" exclaimed Grace's mother. "You are seriously out of line, Mr. Yates, and I will not have you lying about my children. Let go of Grace this instant." Her mother grabbed Grace out of his arms. She demanded that Wilson, their loyal and friendly groundskeeper, in their employ since Grace could remember, leave immediately and not return.

Grace had been sad that Wilson was gone. She missed running into him when she was playing in the yard. He would make her laugh with one of his silly jokes and then reach a gnarled, scarred hand into his tweed jacket pocket and pull out a foil-wrapped Mint Imperial. He always had those mints.

Why had Morvin hated her so much? It had taken a long time for Grace to realize that it was nothing she had done to deserve such torment and ill-treatment over so many years. She had merely been born, and that was enough.

A sudden crack of thunder brought Grace back from her memories. Rain began teeming down on her. She turned to head back to the house when she noticed a figure in the mist about twenty yards away. The long shadows of the early morning made the unkempt grounds appear sinister. She wasn't sure if her eyes were playing tricks or if someone was there watching her. The rain splattered her face as she squinted into the gloom. It looked like the same shape, the same hooded person from when she'd first arrived. The two stood there frozen, looking at each other, his face obscured by the misty downpour predawn light. Then, suddenly, he sprung at her, full tilt, running.

Grace gasped and ran into the back garden with the hope of losing him in some overgrown rhododendrons. The bushes were so massive you couldn't tell where one ended and another began. She tried to navigate without falling over the thick stumps and tangled branches. Panic was quickly setting in though, and a frantic pace was taking over. Her foot jammed under an upturned root, and Grace went down hard, smashing her head on something sticking up out of the ground. She tried to ignore the flash of brilliant pain and struggled back to her feet. Branches scraped her arms and face. She was too terrified to look behind her.

Is it Keaton trying to scare me? But the figure looked huskier than him. She thought about stopping and just confronting him, standing her ground. But the closing sound of his thundering footfalls and his hulking body smashing through the thick brambles made her keep moving.

One of the thick branches snagged Grace's sweater.

She struggled and pulled at it, but it had her firmly in its gnarly grasp. She managed to finally wriggle herself free just as a large hand reached out to grab her. She screamed and bent down, evading his clutches and ran with a fresh burst of adrenaline.

Suddenly free of the rhododendrons and in a clearing, she could see the ancient estate graveyard just ahead. Not risking a glance behind her, she tore through the iron archway and weaved in and out among the old tombstones. Large droplets of rain fell, and darkness closed in, the latter brought on quickly by heavy black clouds and foggy mist. A strong wind began to blow.

Grace was far from the house now; she hadn't been in the cemetery for so long she'd almost forgotten it existed. Along with some of Grace's ancestors were the ancient graves of the Craigrook family that built and lived at the estate long before the Calhouns. Some of the graves dated back as far as the 1600s. Many of the large headstones had all but disappeared into the earth after so many years.

Grace was out of breath. She knew she had to stop soon. Her clothes were becoming heavy with rain, and she couldn't keep up this pace much longer. Blood trickled into her eye from the gash in her forehead. She weaved through a few more tombstones and statues. She ducked behind a large granite headstone that had managed to remain somewhat erect in the many years of earth movement and erosion.

She crouched, listened, and tried to slow her breath without gasping loudly. The din of increasing wind and pelting rain helped to mask her heavy breathing. She couldn't hear any footsteps or any human movement.

Maybe she'd managed to lose him. Grace didn't want to risk peeking over the headstone. *Just wait a while*, she told herself. *Be quiet, and catch your breath.*

She didn't know how much time had passed; it felt like a good ten minutes. Her legs were getting tingly from staying in the crouch position, but she was still too afraid to make any movement. She had to move them soon though, to get some blood flow. Without much noise, she managed to get down on her knees. She couldn't stay out here all day in this weather. The freezing gale cut right through her.

Grace wiped at the blood on her face. She was bleeding heavily.

Is he still out there? Maybe he gave up and left. Or he's trying to outwait me, waiting for me to make the first move.

She searched the ground for a stick or a rock, something to use as a weapon. Her vision blurred from rain and blood. Is that a rock? Grace reached in front of her and grabbed hold of the object. It began to wriggle in her fingers as she realized it was a huge spider. Her gaze traveled up her arm; her skin was moving. She screamed and got up, wiping away at the hundreds of spiders crawling all over her!

She was running backward and just about fell as her foot sunk into the uneven ground all around her. She managed to stay upright, still screaming and frantically rubbing at herself and shaking out her hair.

She turned around abruptly and ran head first right into his hard, broad chest. In the throes of fear and panic Grace flailed in all directions, punching, hitting, and screaming!

"Leave me alone, you bastard! What the hell do you want from me?"

He tried to hold back her flying fists. "Grace! Grace, stop. Stop, it's me. It's Cameron."

"What?" She stopped, opened her eyes. "Oh my god, Cameron." She fell into his arms. "Someone was chasing me. Did you see him?" Then she remembered, and yelled, "Do I have spiders on me?" She danced around in front of him, turning in circles.

"No. No, I don't see anything. Who was chasing you? You're bleeding. Come on. We're pretty close to my place. It's just over that ridge."

Her legs shook, and her chest hurt. Cameron held most of her body weight as they walked. He led her up the hill and eventually ended up carrying her into the warm safety of his cottage.

CHAPTER TWENTY

"HERE'S A CHANGE of clothes. They're going to be huge on you, but they're warm, and they're dry." He directed her to his bedroom to change while he built a fire in the large inglenook fireplace.

Grace couldn't stop shivering. As she undressed, she looked around the handsome room. She'd been here once as a child with her father. It was pretty run-down at that time, but in the last few years, new owners had restored it. It was built in the late 1800s, Grace remembered, and it had all the quaint imperfections of the period but with modern plumbing, heating, and lighting.

The red flannel shirt he gave her was soft and smelled like fresh laundry. He had also given her some thermal long johns. *These are going to look so flattering*, she thought, *especially with the hunting socks*. She noticed a picture of an attractive woman by his bedside and was surprised to find herself upset that he might be married.

She dried her hair with a towel and went back into the inviting living room, while Cameron took her wet clothes and carted them off to the laundry. Grace heard the comforting sound of a dryer begin tumbling. The cottage had a profoundly soothing, cozy ambiance.

"Who's this handsome man?" she asked, as a gorgeous yellow Lab wiggled over to her and introduced himself. He followed her to the fireplace, which was already thoroughly warming the room. She knelt by the hearth and petted the dog, who wagged his tail with enthusiasm.

"This is Piper, my best mate," he said, rubbing the big dog's ears. "And Piper, this is Grace, the beautiful woman I told you about."

Grace felt her face warm. This man was so charming.

"Have a seat by the fire, then, and I'll make you nice hot cuppa."

"Tea would be amazing. Thank you, Cameron." Grace sat down in the puffy recliner in front of the fire. On the table beside it was a pair of reading glasses and an Ian Rankin novel. The fire crackled and sparked, giving the room a glowing warmth. "You could serve dinner in this fireplace. It's stunning."

From the kitchen, he replied, "Aye, I think it's my favorite aspect of the old place."

Cameron came back into the room and covered her lap with a thick, wool tartan blanket. He had a wet cloth in his hands.

"Tea's brewing. Let's take a look at that forehead," he said, as he leaned over her. "Bleeding has slowed down, thank goodness." He dabbed gently at her wound. She drew a little breath through her teeth and winced.

"Sorry, lass, but it'll have to be cleaned and dressed." He looked into her eyes, and she saw kindness in his that turned her heart to jelly. He smelled so good, like Christmas, comforting, clean, and warm. She felt a sudden urge to run her fingers through his brown, wavy hair as he looked down and adjusted the cloth.

"What happened out there, Grace? Who was after ye?"

She could listen to him say 'Grrrace' all day long. "I don't know who it was. It's the same hooded person that scared me the evening I arrived at Craighouse. I do know it's not my nephew. This man is way bigger. And I can handle that skinny Keaton."

He left the room to get the tea, talking as he went. "Well, it sounds like you're in danger to me."

"I think someone's just trying to scare me. I definitely won't be going outside by myself anymore though, that's for sure."

Piper laid down right on top of Grace's feet and looked up at her with big, brown eyes. *Okay,* thought Grace, *I'm officially a sucker for the both of you.*

"Here we are," he said. "A tray of hot tea and biscuits for two." He placed the tray on the coffee table. "Are you a sweet and white or just sweet," he chuckled. "Well, I already know you're very sweet." He winked at her.

He had a cute grin, with amazing dimples and eyes that smiled. He had a muscular build but was lean and quite tall.

"Just milk, please. I truly appreciate all this, Cameron. I hope I'm not too much of an inconvenience."

He handed her the tea and offered a cookie. "You're a much-needed distraction today. I'm a little stalled with the novel for some reason. Piper seems to have accepted your presence with no hesitation at all. Look at him. He's in love we ye already."

She looked down at the dog, and he thumped his tail on the floor in agreement. "I think I'm in love with him too." She cleared her throat a little, feeling a bit uneasy after her comment, and sipped her tea. It tasted heavenly, just what she needed.

"The cottage is charming. How often do you come back here?" Grace asked.

"Em, I usually try to write a book at least every couple of years, so I'm up here every eighteen months or so. I come here a lot more since my wife passed away."

"I'm so sorry. May I ask what happened?"

Cameron shifted a little on the settee and looked into the fire, "It's been five years now...cancer." He looked back at Grace. "How about you, are you married?" He stood up to tend the fire, bending down by her legs.

"No, I'm starting to think it's just not in my cards."

"Ach, away," he said. His Scottish slang reminded her so much of her father. "You're young yet," he continued, poking the wood around, "and very lovely as well."

Things went a bit quiet then, and Grace didn't know what to say. She searched her mind for something appropriate. "Well, Piper and I think you look pretty good too."

He smiled at that, "Pretty good? That's it? Is that all I get Piper, you big, bad boy?" He grabbed his dog and began wrestling with him on the floor.

Grace laughed as the two jostled around. This was

nice; she needed a break from the madness she'd been dealing with at the house.

"Ready for more tea? Or is it time for something a little stronger? You look like you could use two fingers of the good stuff. Nothin' like a good wee snort to calm yoursel' and warm yer belly." He went to a beautiful oak and brass sideboard with well-carved galleons running along the top, obviously original with the cottage, and poured two drams of Glenfiddich.

"Only if I can come and take a look at your kitchen. I'm so curious about this old place."

He went over and extended his forearm down to her. She grabbed hold, and he heaved her to her feet.

The kitchen had been extensively renovated and had all the modern amenities. They kept the stone walls and flooring original, though, along with the timber beams that ran through the ceiling. The result was a unique balance between modern beauty and rugged historical elegance.

He gave a full tour of the small cottage with a stop in the bathroom to dress her forehead. She enjoyed having his face so close to hers as he applied a bandage to her head.

He showed her the den, where he spent much of his time. It was tidy and organized. It had a couch for Cameron that he used to get horizontal at times when his muse took the day off. And it also had a big, comfy dog bed for Piper, which he immediately occupied.

"Why 'Piper,' just out of curiosity?" Grace asked.

Cameron took a sip of his scotch before answering. "I used to play. Well, I mean, I still do, occasionally. I just don't compete anymore."

Grace couldn't help herself and immediately had him

pictured in the full regalia, kilt and all. The vision had her feeling more than a little intrigued.

"I love bagpipes. You'll play for me one day, I hope." She realized that this would mean seeing each other again and hoped it wasn't too presumptuous. She was beginning to like this smart, kind, delicious Scotsman a lot.

"Sure," he said, without hesitation. "I'd be honored."

Why did every word out of his mouth make her knees go weak? Grace took the last sip of her scotch as the dryer buzzed in the distance, announcing its completion.

"Well, Cameron, I guess I should be going. I've taken up too much of your time already."

"I can't think of any way I'd rather spend my time," he smiled at her. "Will you let me walk you back, though? And I'd like to get your number, you know, in case you need help again."

"Of course, thank you. Oh, I forgot. My cell phone has mysteriously disappeared."

"Well, you can't be without one. Here, take mine for now. I've got a landline if I need it. You can reach me here, just in case." He handed her his expensive-looking cell.

"Thanks again, it seems that's all I ever say to you." She hated looking so helpless. *He must think I'm so weak,* she thought. Hopefully, she'd get the chance to show him otherwise and also repay his kindness.

Grace changed back into her clothes and met Cameron at the door. It was approximately a fifteen-minute walk between Grace's house and the cottage, through a mixture of forest and field. The conversation came easy as they went, and the odd small silence filled with a noticeable charge between them.

"Earlier, you said someone was trying to scare you. Why would anyone want to do that?" Cameron asked.

"Well, it's kind of a long, sordid story. My mother recently passed away—"

"Oh, I'm sorry," he interrupted.

"Thank you. Anyway, it turns out that my mum left everything to me, the whole bloody lot, and my sister is furious about it." Grace kept her head down as she talked. It felt good to be able to share her ordeal with someone. She didn't want to call Devi. She'd be on the next train.

"I think I've seen your sister. Has she got long, bright red hair?" Cameron asked as he bent to pick up a stick. He threw it ahead of them for Piper, who bounded after it at full speed.

"Yes, that's her. Her son has the same, flaming red locks. His isn't quite as long...or as clean, I might add. I'm just not sure what's going on in that house. I don't know if I'm over exaggerating things or if I'm in real danger. I feel so open, hopeless, at the mercy of people that strongly despise me." Grace looked up at him as they walked to check his expression. Was she honestly asking for this man's help? Grace barely knew him, and was his help truly necessary? After all this time surviving on her own, she couldn't believe she felt so vulnerable. "I'm so embarrassed to lay all this on you. I'm really not 'the damsel in distress' type...honest."

"I'm here, anytime, whatever you need," he nodded at her and grinned, but his eyes were worried.

Piper ran back to Cameron with the stick in his mouth and dropped it at his feet, then bounced back and forth from his front to his back legs, asking for another go. Cameron was too involved in the conversation and didn't notice.

The happy Lab knew the way well and never let too much distance get between him and his master. He did spy a rabbit, at one point, and took off like a bullet but was soon right back at Cameron's side, tongue lolling and tail wagging.

"So, you think it's them that are trying to scare you into leaving?" he asked. They were approaching the estate now.

"Yes, I do. I've told Morvin that I don't intend to keep the money. I don't want one penny of it. There's so much more to it, though. We've never gotten along." *That's an understatement*, she thought.

Cameron walked her right to the mansion's front steps.

"This place is magnificent," he said, looking up at the stately home.

"Well, it used to be. In need of some major TLC these days, I'm afraid," said Grace.

He looked at Grace and took her hand in his. Her insides tingled, her heart beat in double time.

"Well, you be careful, lass. Anything *oot of* the ordinary and you call me. Do not hesitate. I'm worried for ye. Ye know that." He kissed the back of her hand.

"Okay, Cameron, I will. Umm, I'd like to see you again though, even if nothing transpires here. And I need to return your phone anyway." There, she said it. She raised her eyebrows, hoping for a positive response.

"I'd like that too. How about if I call and check in wi' ye' tomorrow, then?" he asked.

"Perfect."

Grace watched from the window as Cameron and Piper headed back down the long driveway. She smiled, enjoying the view, as she thought about how good it felt in his company.

She was already looking forward to seeing him again.

CHAPTER TWENTY-ONE

THE LOUD BELL of the old rotary telephone began ringing as Grace was ascending the stairs to her room. Its shrill was so loud you could hear it all the way upstairs from its location at the other end of the mansion. *Is no one going to answer it?* she wondered. *It must have rung six times by now.* On about the eighth ring, Grace decided to run for it. It could be the hospital concerning Aunt Lena.

"Hello?" Grace answered the phone, a little out of breath. It was Charlie Patterson; he owned the local nursery in town. "Hi Charlie, how're you? How's business?" Grace asked. Morvin had worked for the small nursery since as far back as Grace could remember. As a teenager, Charlie had offered Grace a part-time job as well. She liked the summer position as a cashier but never developed a passion for plants like her sister.

"Is that Gracey? I guess you're in town for your mother's funeral. So sorry to hear about that darlin', we were just sickened by the news. She was always such a strong woman, your mum." Charlie was a sweet man. He and his wife Jess had been married forever. They both worked very hard to keep their little family business afloat.

"Thank you, Charlie," said Grace. She took a seat on the stool by the phone. "It's been quite a shock, for sure."

"Gracey, the reason I'm calling is that Jess is clearing out the old supply shed. We've been neglecting that place for years, and she came across a chemical that we're not sure about. We don't know where it came from. It's not anywhere in the order book, but a slip on the bottle has Morvin's initials on it. So we're hoping maybe she can shed some light on it. Hey, I made a pun there. Get it? In the shed...shed some light, ha-ha."

Grace envisioned the deep crow's feet on his round face as he laughed.

"Good one, Charlie," Grace laughed back. "What's it called? I'll ask her when she gets back from the store." Grace looked on the counter for a pen and paper.

"Thanks, love. It's called methyl iodide. They use it in some of those industrial plant fields, but we've never had use for it here. Pretty toxic stuff, not good to keep hanging 'round."

"Okay, I'll have her call you," Grace said after writing it down. "Please say hi to Jess for me."

"I will do, dear, but you'll have to come by for tea and say hello. It's been ages since we've seen your pretty face."

"I'll try and get down there to see you real soon, Charlie."

They said their goodbyes and Grace hung up the

phone. *Strange,* she thought. She remembered reading about a tragic accident involving the same chemical at one of the field plantations upcountry last year. A man driving a tractor had accidentally unearthed the toxic liquid, releasing it into his airspace. He died soon after from complications to his central nervous system. Why would Morvin have ordered such a poisonous chemical to a little family-run nursery? And where the heck was she anyway?

Grace looked around the house for any sign of her sister or nephew. She called out their names a couple of times and felt a little spooked at the empty echoes in the old dusty corridors. Nothing. *Okay,* she thought, *time for a little more snooping around the old house then, starting with Morvin's bedroom.* Grace wasn't even sure what she was looking for, but things were off around here. Something was going on, and Grace knew Morvin had everything to do with it.

Morvin's room was the same one she'd had when they were young. It was on the second floor but at the opposite end of the house from Grace's. As Grace neared Morvin's wing, the smell of must and age grew. It was even more potent as Grace entered the airless bedroom. The large door seemed to moan loudly, as if in pain. It echoed through the house, announcing Grace's secret invasion of Morvin's privacy.

Wow, thought Grace, *she does not believe in updating, that's for sure.* Grace drew her sweater tighter around her shoulders and rubbed her arms. *I guess blood-sucking vampires don't need heat. Now, I wonder where the coffin is.*

The room was an homage to the nineteenth century. Dark weighty furnishings, lace doilies that would probably turn to dust if you touched them. The walls were covered in faded floral wallpaper of once rich browns and golds, yuck. She felt like she had just entered a scene out of one of her favorite 1930s mystery novels by Daphne DuMaurier. Complete with pouring rain pelting at the window and the sound of a howling wind promising a nasty storm on the way.

Grace headed to the small writing table by the window that overlooked the rolling fields at the north end of the estate. She sat down on the red velvet stool. Grace remembered the lush deep fabric had been quite pretty in its day, but now the velvet had rubbed away in places leaving it looking shabby and worn.

She found nothing of note on top of the desk, nor the first drawer. The one underneath was locked. After some quick deliberation, Grace grabbed a letter opener and easily pried the cheap lock open.

She was stunned at what she found. Piles and piles of letters and cards all bound together in two bundles with rough butchers twine. Grace recognized a few things in one of the collections: birthday cards, Christmas cards, and letters that Grace had sent to her mother over the years. She felt her heart start to pound heavily in her chest. The other bundle was full of the same, but these were cards and letters *from* her mother to her! Grace's mouth suddenly became dry, and she felt physically ill. This discovery meant her mother did care about her, loved her. It changed everything Grace ever felt about her mother, about her home.

"Just what the hell do you think you're doing in here?"

A rock dropped in Grace's stomach. She whirled around to face her sister.

"I can't fucking believe you!" spat Grace. Morvin was standing in the doorway, visibly shaking. "Why didn't I get all these letters?

"You didn't deserve them. Mother should never have written one of them to you. You never did anything for her," Morvin said.

"And these?" Grace held out the stack sent from her in England. "I suppose she never even saw one of these?"

"I should have burned them all," Morvin sneered. She began approaching Grace, her hand outstretched, intending to take the letters from her.

"Why? Why would you do this? All this time I thought Mum had just written me off. It killed me. And here, all along, she was writing to me? You're nothing but a sour, manipulative, old bitch!" Grace stormed out of the room, taking the letters with her, overwhelmed by the mix of hurt and anger. She yelled at Morvin over her shoulder, "You'll burn in hell for this. I'm going to see you never get a dime of Mother's money!"

CHAPTER TWENTY-TWO

I CAN'T BELIEVE MY lame sister doesn't have any internet service, thought Grace, as she drove. After the heated argument in Morvin's room, Grace hid the pile of letters in her bedroom and then jumped in her car. She'd find out what methyl iodide was on her own, without asking Morvin.

Grace pulled her car into the library parking lot. She used to love coming here when she was young. Not only did the old building contain books, which always made Grace happy, but the structure itself was gloriously ancient. It was built in 1883 and was an excellent example of Victorian Gothic Revival architecture. It had undergone some quite extensive maintenance, repair, and renovations over the years, but the original face of the building and many of the ornate and period details had been respectfully preserved. Land developers these days were sometimes all too quick to demolish a gorgeous, historical building.

A sudden crack of thunder frightened Grace as she approached the library steps. The sky had grown steadily darker and more ominous on the drive over. She made it to the door just as heavy rain began to pelt against the concrete.

Grace headed for the non-fiction, reference section, noting as she walked that thankfully, not much in the old library had changed in all these years. The massive white pillars still stood by the checkout counters, and those sweet little wrought iron Juliet balconies that ran the length of each side wall also remained.

Many times within these ancient walls, Grace had happily lost herself in these books, researching times long past or gaining historical insight for one of her future bestsellers. She would stroll the many aisles where wars, deaths, births, legacies, and fellowships beseeched her attention at every turn. After collecting a few well-chosen tomes, she would find a private alcove and immerse herself in the flavor of the era. Enjoying not only the historical facts inside, but also the books' weight in her hands, the musky smell of their bindings, the divine crackle of their spines when opened.

The library was quiet, so Grace had her choice of computers to use. She sat down at one and began to look up the chemical Charlie asked about.

"Okay," Grace said as she browsed, "here it is. 'Methyl iodide is a chemical compound that is a dense, colorless, volatile liquid.' Upon further reading, she learned that it was a commonly used pesticide for pre-plant soil treatment. Grace scrolled down a bit to a section on Toxicity.

'If inhaled, ingested, or even absorbed by the skin, it

can cause headache, sudden onset of slurred speech, double vision, and lack of muscle movement. This can be limited to one side of the body.'

Grace sat back in her chair, eyes widening in shock.

"Oh my God," Grace said aloud, "these are all stroke-like symptoms."

"I beg your pardon?" said a scowling woman, seated at the computer beside her.

"Oh, nothing. Sorry." She closed her eyes and slowly shook her head in disbelief. *Is this possible? Did Morvin really do this? Poison both their mother and aunt? Why Aunt Lena though? Maybe she was onto Morvin, and that's what Lena was trying to tell me in the hospital, why she was so agitated.*

Grace read on, 'High dose acute toxicity includes kidney failure, brain injury, arterial blood clotting, seizures, and coma.'

"Oh my God," Grace said again. She sent the page to the printer, closed the tab, and gathered her things.

"Grace? Grace Calhoun? Is that you?"

Grace turned around to the dry, cracked voice behind her.

"It is you. My goodness, it's been years."

"Mrs. Hargraves?" Lydia Hargraves was a long-time friend of Grace's mother and the head librarian. Well, back then she was; she must have retired by now. Grace hadn't seen her for at least eighteen years.

Lydia wrapped a skinny arm around Grace and squeezed her tight. Grace returned the affection. After the embrace, Mrs. Hargraves still held Grace by the hand.

"Wow, it's been so long. How are you? Are you still working here?" Grace asked.

"I'm doing fine, dear. Mr. Hargraves passed a few years

ago now. They let me volunteer here in the library a few days a week. Honestly, I'd go batty if I didn't have this place to keep my mind going."

The old librarian still wore her hair the same way—up in a severely tight bun—and still had the same brown Kirby grips scattered throughout. "How about you, Gracey? You married? I was so sad when you lost touch with your mum. How is she these days?"

"Oh, um," Grace stammered a little, not wanting to blurt it out and shock the poor old woman. "She actually just passed away very recently."

"What? No. What happened?" Lydia hugged Grace again.

"The doctors say it was her heart."

"Bollocks!" Lydia announced, quite loudly, breaking her own rule of quiet in the library. "I just saw your mum last year at the fundraiser. She looked in fine fettle. I can't believe it."

"Yes, I know. Apparently, Mum took ill and then had a heart attack in the hospital." Grace saw tears well up in Lydia's eyes.

"So, I guess that sister of yours is chomping at the bit for the money then, eh?" Lydia's temperament changed from sad to angry. "I'm sorry, but that son of hers is a menace. He's no good that one. Can you believe he got away with what he did to the Stimson's?"

"I'm afraid I don't know what you're talking about. What did Keaton do, Mrs. Hargraves?"

"Oh, it's Lydia, dear. You're all grown up now...and very lovely." She smiled at Grace, kindness once more in her eyes but short-lived as she continued. "Well, old Mr. Stimson, you know, out at the Fletcher place? He complained to the police about Keaton and his mates. They're always partying loudly well into the night, and leaving litter all over behind his house." Lydia took Grace by the arm and led her to a corner of the library, looking periodically behind as if she didn't want anyone overhearing her gossiping. "So, it seems that when the police looked into it, they found a bunch of stolen merchandise hidden behind the property and Keaton got in some trouble there. I guess Keaton was angry at Stimson, so he set fire to his house. Someone actually saw him doing it and called it in before the fire killed the old man."

Grace couldn't believe what she was hearing. Lydia wasn't done yet, though.

"Your sister was irate. She hired some fancy lawyer, and he actually got Keaton off of all charges. Not so much as a slap on the wrist!" Lydia's voice was rising again, and she clapped her hand over her mouth.

"That's terrible! I had no idea." Grace knew the boy was troubled, but arson, with the intent to hurt or even kill someone? Unbelievable.

"You should be careful around him, Grace. Your sister turns a blind eye, she doesn't know what he's capable of."

Grace agreed that she'd watch herself. The two hugged one last time before Grace headed for the exit.

The rain outside was now a deluge. The twenty or so steps to her car had Grace completely drenched. She fumbled for her keys as the rain pounded.

"Damn it." She dropped her keys in a puddle beside the door, and as she bent to get them noticed a car across the lot with its high beams on. They seemed to be shining right on her.

CHAPTER TWENTY-THREE

"'FILL YOU UP, Mr. Elliot?" the waitress asked with a flutter of her eyelashes.

"Aye, please," Cameron said, nodding.

"How was your run this morning? Quite cool out. Um, you've got something on your jacket there." She leaned over and brushed a bit of sand off his shoulder, and then, deliberately, made close eye contact with him as she moved back.

"Oh, Piper and I did a bit of wrestling on the beach. How's he doing out there?" Cameron looked over to his right through the window, missing her advance completely, and saw his dog resting faithfully on the step.

Most mornings, usually at the crack of dawn, one could find Cameron and Piper running along Durham beach. After a brisk forty-minute jaunt, they always stopped for a few rounds of fetch, before their daily stop at 'The Tea and Toast.'

Discouraged, but not surprised that her efforts, once again, went unnoticed, Carla kept at it.

"Working on your book, I see," she said, peeking at his notes. "Can I read what you've got so far?" She rubbed her fingers lightly, seductively at her cleavage, and gave him a wink.

Cameron always took his notebook on his runs. There was a steep, craggy hill above the beach, and at the top stood the remains of an old sept. The view of the North Atlantic from the church ruins was always a source of inspiration for Cameron and his trusty Moleskin.

Cameron moved his hand quickly to close the book and hide his private notes, inadvertently knocking his coffee, spilling some on the table.

"Whoops," she said. "I'll get that." She took the opportunity to lean over and give him another chance to look at her large breasts.

"It's okay. I've got it," he said, stopping her. "There's not much, thank goodness." Cameron wiped at the little spill with his elbow. He noticed a slightly rotund, balding man flailing one arm in the air a few tables down. "Carla, I think that fellow over there is trying to wave you down."

Discouraged again, Carla walked over to the flabby arm, wiggling in the air. After refilling a coffee, she went back behind the counter and leaned on the pick-up window.

"What do I have to do? Jump up and down naked in front of that guy to get his attention?" she asked Jerry, the cook.

"It's worth a try, I guess. Do me a favor, though, and let me know if you do. I'll make sure I take my break and catch the show as well." He laughed and slapped the pick-up bell.

Carla rolled her eyes at him and picked up a hot plate of streaky bacon and fried eggs. As she delivered the meal over to table four, she barely took her eyes off her favorite, albeit oblivious, customer.

Cameron got up and walked to the cash register. Carla rushed over, eager for another opportunity to chat with the rich, handsome author. Cameron was preoccupied, though, apparently listening in on a conversation between three young men seated at the counter beside the register.

"Is she at least a babe, this aunt of yours?" asked the pimply one.

One of them had a head of fiery red hair and was very fidgety, continually looking behind him and shaking his left leg. "I guess she's okay if you're old. She's a fucking bitch, though," he said. "Thinks she can just come here, out of the blue, and take over. She's inheriting everything, man. I need the money way more than she does."

"Not much you can do about it if it's in the will," said Pimply.

"Oh, there's something I can do about it. Make her want to leave and if that doesn't work, make her disappear," said Red.

"You probably would, you sick pup," said the third one at the table.

"Shit. I gotta go, my mum needs her car back by eleven." Pimply got up from the table.

Cameron finished paying and handed Carla a fiver. "Thanks, Carla. See you tomorrow."

"Can't wait," she said, with a wink and a sexy smile.

"Hey, do you know those jokers?" Cameron asked her

quietly, gesturing with his head in the direction of the three young men.

"Them? Yeah, they're regulars, but they're usually here later in the day. Bunch of losers, always hitting on me, and they never leave a tip."

Cameron thanked her again and left the diner. He stood outside with Piper, who was having one last go at the bowl of fresh water the restaurant always provided. When Piper had enough, he walked over to Cameron, dribbling about a gallon of water all over Cameron's feet.

"Hey! Thanks a lot for that, buddy," he said with a chuckle and rubbed Piper's ears. Cameron looked up as the door to the diner opened and the three men he had been listening to filed out.

"Hey you," said Cameron, up close and personal to the redhead. "I heard you in there talking about hurting someone. I think I know who you were talking about, and I'm telling you to stay away from her. You so much as lay one finger on her, and you'll be answering to me."

"Take it easy, old man. I don't know what the hell you're talking about. Get the hell out my way." Keaton shoved past Cameron and headed to the parking lot.

"I'm telling you, punk. Leave Grace alone!" Cameron yelled after them.

The three kept walking and got in their car. Cameron kept watching as they drove out of the lot. As they sped past, the tires screaming on the asphalt, he noticed that Pimply was giving him the finger.

CHAPTER TWENTY-FOUR

THE FRIGID AIR inside the car was biting and she saw her breath as she put the papers on the passenger seat. She turned the ignition and held herself tightly, waiting for the car to warm up.

"I really must invest in some new wipers," said Grace as she squinted through the pelting rain on her windshield. Visibility was next to nil as she exited the parking lot. She took a right onto Carlisle Street and noticed high beams again, this time coming up fast in her rearview mirror.

"What's with you?" Grace said out loud.

The car began tailing her bumper closely. Thankfully, Grace was taking another right turn at the next block.

"See ya' later, psycho," she said.

She rounded the corner and checked her mirror. The car stayed on her tail. Now feeling a little unnerved, she sped up cautiously; her old VW didn't handle all that well in the best of weather, never mind in a torrential downpour.

She decided to take another turn with the hope of losing them and felt her rear end fishtail on the bend. The car still followed, almost kissing her back bumper. Now she was downright scared. She pressed the gas harder but had to ease off as she felt a loss of control in the steering wheel. She could barely see out the window, the rain pouring like a river down the glass.

The lights from the houses and cars outside her window blurred past in the wet darkness. Grace saw that she was approaching a traffic light up ahead and prayed it would stay green. She was still a few car lengths before the intersection when the light turned yellow.

"Shit." She was going to have to run the red, but then it occurred to her that the idiot behind her wouldn't make it in time and would have to stop or get hit by cross traffic.

She sped through the yellow light, feeling triumphant but then watched in disbelief as the car swerved violently to avoid an accident and then sped up behind her bumper once more.

Grace couldn't go any faster. She would lose control of the car. She glanced at her rearview again and screamed, just missing a pedestrian crossing the road in front of her. She hit the brakes, felt her car skid, and braced herself for the impact from the car behind. She heard tires screech, and the pedestrian yell as she pressed the gas and sped away. The mysterious driver stayed on her tail.

She took a fast, yet cautious left turn at the next opportunity, finding herself on a desolate stretch of road.

"Where the hell am I?" The insane driver caught up to her and hit her bumper hard. Grace's car jolted from the hit, and she fought hard to correct the swerve of her vehicle. She hastily took an abrupt right turn and nearly slammed into a pole. The driver following couldn't make the turn and had to stay heading straight.

She'd lost them.

She slowed down and caught her breath. "What the hell was that?" Grace had no idea where she was as she tried to read a passing street sign, but it was obscured by the streaming rain. She drove on and made a right at the next street, in the opposite direction of the crazy driver. She was still peering through her window, trying to get her bearings when she saw in horror that he was back behind her. "Oh shit, no!"

The car suddenly passed beside her on the narrow road, and she tried to get a look at the driver but saw only a dark blur through the two wet windows. Grace slammed the brakes as the car swerved madly in front of her and abruptly slid to a stop. She tried frantically to reverse but accidentally stalled her damn car.

"Oh my God, oh my God, please, please, don't let this be happening," Grace prayed. She watched in terror as a towering, hooded figure emerged from the car and walked toward her. Grace glanced at her door locks; the right rear button was up! She tried to reach it with her left hand, twisting her upper body around as far as possible, but it was too far. Her right, of course, didn't straighten and didn't have the strength to push the button down anyway.

Grace instinctively reeled sideways as the steel hilt of a large hunting knife bashed through the glass by her ear, sending an explosion of rain and glass all over her face and lap.

He put his face through the now open window. Grace felt his heavy, hot, snorting breath on her skin.

"You fucking tell that weasel Keaton, he needs to pay up, right?" he said in a strong cockney accent. "And if he don't, by Friday night, I'm going to come into your big bloody house and take it meself, along with a nice big slice of your pale, white skin. *Ye gorrit?*" He ran the flat top of the knife along her cheek.

Grace was frozen, her mouth hanging open, her eyes clenched shut. She managed to nod her head and open her eyes slightly to look at the hostile assailant. He had a massive head with enormous, flaring nostrils. There was a thick, pink scar from the bottom of his right eye all the way to his jawline. His intense eyes bored into hers with the fierceness of a raging madman.

"I don't know anything about any money," Grace said, hoping to reason with the beast. "Maybe there's a misunderstanding here."

"There ain't no fucking misunderstanding, lady. He borrowed from some dangerous people, and it's time for payback. Either he does or you fucking will!"

He pressed the knife harder into her skin, ran it down to her neck and just held it there for a few seconds, still breathing heavily on her. He said nothing further, but his message was clear. Grace was afraid to move, wouldn't dare; it felt like he was trying to decide how far to take this.

Grace decided to chance a response. "Okay," she said. It came out in a whisper. Apparently convinced that she understood, he backed out of the window, walked back to his car, and sped away, leaving a spray of water in his wake.

Grace sat there, shaking. "Holy Jesus! What the *hell* was that?"

Hands shaking, she tried the engine. It started. She checked her cheek and neck for blood; two red marks but no broken skin. She put the car in drive and headed in any direction. She took a series of right turns and then, thankfully, recognized a familiar grocery store.

In a state of shock and horror, she headed for Craigrook, the rain pouring in the broken window, her lap full of glass, and her eyes ever watchful in the rearview.

CHAPTER TWENTY-FIVE

GRACE THANKFULLY ARRIVED home safely but still shaken after her horrific encounter with that awful, deranged man. She'd been intent on telling Morvin what had happened but found that she either wasn't home or was already in bed. So instead, she found some tape and used a garbage bag to seal up her window as best she could. It was quite some feat with the raging wind and sheeting rain.

After that ordeal she couldn't wait to get changed and hole up into the warmth of her bedclothes. She took Cameron's cell phone out of her purse and crawled under the covers. After a couple of rings, Devi answered.

"Grace! Oh my God, we've all been so worried. I've left messages, why haven't you been answering your phone?"

"I can't find it. I borrowed this one from a friend. How're things going?" Grace asked.

"Things are not good, Gracey. There was a fire in the building. The damage wasn't too bad to your shop, but Armin's had to close business for a while."

"What? What about the flat? How bad was it? Is everyone okay? Is Ernie okay?" Grace was stunned by the news.

"Yes, yes, don't worry. Everyone is fine. Like I said, the smoke damage was only to your store and the two shops on either side. They're not sure what started it yet, still investigating. But we were all so worried about you that Marc decided to drive up and check on you. Have you seen him?"

"Marc is here? No, I haven't seen him. When did he leave?" Grace asked.

"Two days ago. That's strange. Maybe he changed his mind. I'll call him. How are you coping though, Grace? How're things going with your sister?" Devi asked.

"There's some weird stuff going on around here. I'll fill you in in a couple of days, Devi. It's late, and I'm exhausted. Thanks again for looking after things for me. Say hi to Wesley and Ernie. I still can't believe his brother coming all the way here...seriously, I'm fine."

"Okay, Grace. I'm so glad you called. Keep in touch, okay?"

"I will. Talk to you soon. Bye, Devi." Grace put the cell phone back in her purse by the bed and flicked off her lamp. *Maybe Marc does really care about me after all,* she thought. She couldn't believe there was a fire in her building. The lack of business was really going to set her finances back, but at least no one was hurt.

She tried to get comfortable and force sleep but knew she was probably in for another rocky night.

It's all her fault, he thought as he watched her sleep. *Everything's just gone right to shit since she showed up.* Keaton could barely see his hands in front of his face as he took another sip of water. He continued to stare at her as she tossed and turned in the bed, and he leaned forward as her nightgown fell off one shoulder. Keaton licked his lips, hoping to see more, feeling aroused at the sight of her bare skin. He couldn't see shit from here, though. Time for a closer look.

He crept to her door, avoiding any creaky spots on the wood floor. He slowly turned the knob and cringed as it let out a light metal scrape. He pushed open the door and entered Grace's room. Stepping as lightly as possible, he approached her bedside, although the storm outside was an excellent muffler to his movements. He stood over her form and damned the darkness. It was hard to see anything very well. Grace muttered something and moved onto her side, bringing the blankets up to her neck. *Dammit*, he thought.

He slithered over to her bureau and slowly pulled out the top drawer, all the while keeping an eye on her for any sign of movement. Jackpot. He found exactly what he was looking for...panties.

Keaton took out a dark pair, he couldn't see what color they were but secretly hoped they were red. He put them to his nose and inhaled Grace's scent. He felt himself getting aroused and smelled them again, reveling in the thought of what he was doing; she didn't know he was here, yet he was only feet away from her hot body. Stupid bitch. His erection grew.

Keaton looked at the armchair by her bed and had a sudden epiphany; he could actually solve all their problems right now, his and his mother's. He walked over to the chair and grabbed the puffy, over-sized cushion on top of it. He carried it over to the bed, his arousal even stronger in anticipation of what he was about to do. Keaton stood poised for a few moments and was just about to press the pillow to her face, readying himself for her struggle, when he heard a whisper from the doorway.

"Keaton."

Jesus, it was Mother. He scowled at her, waved her away with his arm, and mouthed the words, "Get out."

She motioned strongly for him to come to her. She too was scowling in the dark.

Grace stirred and changed her position, making Keaton duck down slightly, afraid she was waking. He shook his head at his mother but replaced the pillow and walked toward her in the doorway. He quietly closed the door behind them, and they walked swiftly to Morvin's room.

"Not tonight, Keaton, my dear. There is a better way."

CHAPTER TWENTY-SIX

SHE'D BEEN AWAKE for hours after another restless night. Thankfully, as darkness finally began lifting in her room, Grace put on her robe and plodded tiredly to the kitchen. Morvin was already seated at the table, reading the paper. The dim light of another gloomy morning only added to the frigid atmosphere of the room. She could feel Morvin's eyes on her, could sense Morvin judging her every movement as Grace stirred milk into her tea. She sat down across from Morvin, who was still staring at her over her reading glasses.

After a sip of her hot tea, Grace cleared her throat.

"I need to talk to you about Keaton," Grace said.

Morvin ignored her and went back to her newspaper.

"Morvin, he's in some serious trouble with money. I was physically threatened by an angry, dangerous man yesterday."

Morvin slowly looked over her glasses again and sneered.

"Aunt Lena's dead," she said in a flat voice.

"What?" Grace abruptly stood up and knocked over her cup. Tea spilled all over the table.

"Jesus Christ, Grace. Look what you've done! Still a complete gimp, I see." Morvin got up to get a dishrag.

Grace thought back to the hundreds of times Morvin had used that word...gimp. All the memories of the torment, the years of abuse she had endured from her sister came rushing back. She felt seven years old again, small, insignificant, and stupid. "I'm sorry, it was just the shock. When did it happen?" she asked.

"I don't know," Morvin shrugged one shoulder. "Yesterday, I think."

"Yesterday? Why didn't you tell me?" Grace's voice was rising.

Morvin threw the dishrag into the puddle of tea, splashing it all over Grace's blouse. "I just did. Clean up your mess. My god, you really are an idiot, you'll never change. How do you even function day to day without a brain? Be careful you don't break that cup and go out and get me a new paper." Morvin let out an exhausted sigh. "What'll you do for your next act? Set fire to the house? Idiot."

Grace looked at the stain on her blouse and felt rage building inside her.

"It was an accident, Morvin. Stop treating me like a child. I will not put up with it. I'm not a little girl anymore you can push around anytime you feel like it." Grace began to sop up the spill.

"My, oh my. Well, looky here. Little mousey thinks she has a voice," Morvin mocked. "You know where the door is, princess. You don't like it? Do us all a huge favor and leave!"

Grace felt the familiar sting from her sister's words and was about to impulsively react like a wounded child. Instead, she paused, took a breath, and fixed her shoulders. *No, Grace, you can stand up to her.* She moved closer to Morvin, getting right in her face.

"Something very wrong has been going on around here, and I know you're at the bottom of it all. I'm going to prove it, and you're going to pay. You're a sick woman, Morvin." Grace was breathing heavily and shaking inside.

Morvin's face reddened. She looked like a bomb about to explode. Her face went tight, and her lips pulled back from her teeth. Then, suddenly, the muscles in her face relaxed, her shoulders softened.

"I have absolutely no idea what you're talking about, Gracey," she almost sang the words. "I mean, I know things have been difficult since you got back. We just need to calm down, sort some things out. And we've got a lot of arrangements to make." She took the rag from Grace and finished wiping up the mess herself. "Maybe we should do that over dinner tonight. I'm making rice pudding for dessert. I remembered just this morning that used to be your favorite." She looked at Grace with a cold, strange grin. "Oh, and don't worry about the paper, I was nearly finished reading it anyway."

"Um...what? Dinner?" Grace said, taken aback by the abrupt change in Morvin's personality. "I don't think so." *No way will I trust anything you cook,* thought Grace.

"All right. I'll leave the pudding in the fridge for you.

You really must try it, though. Promise me?" She wrung out the rag in the sink and left it on the counter.

"Have you come across my cell phone?" Grace asked. "I seem to have misplaced it."

She had barely finished her question when Morvin answered quickly, "No."

"And, has someone come around looking for me? A man, good-looking, around thirty?"

"No." Again with the abrupt, simple answer. Then, without another word, Morvin walked out of the kitchen.

What the hell was that?

Morvin just kept walking, slowly, straight-backed, all the way to the end of the hall. Then she stopped and stood there, doing nothing for at least a full minute, staring at the wall. Then she turned around and looked at Grace but said nothing. In the dark, shadowy hallway, she looked like a big, looming vulture.

"Morvin?" Grace said. "Are you okay?"

She stood there for another few long seconds. Grace felt chilled, unnerved. Then Morvin simply turned right and walked into one of the guest bedrooms.

CHAPTER TWENTY-SEVEN

"WOW. WHAT A scene." Grace went up to her room after the strange confrontation with Morvin and laid down on her bed. Morvin had acted so queerly. *Maybe there's something seriously wrong with her. Besides being a sadistic, cruel psychopath.*

Grace tried to get some of the facts she had uncovered straight in her mind. It appeared that Morvin had used the water hemlock from her garden to poison and murder their mother. Why? Then, it seems, she used a poisonous chemical to kill their Aunt Lena because she found out. She had also learned that Keaton was in dangerous trouble with money lenders. *Okay, Morvin would do anything for her son, right? So, maybe she wanted to be rid of Mother to free up the inheritance to help him out of his mess. Sick.*

She sat up on the side of the bed, slumped her

shoulders and closed her eyes. It was all so bewildering, upsetting, and surreal. When she opened her eyes again, her gaze fell upon the old children's book she had found in her mother's room. She picked it up and opened the fragile cloth cover.

It was in reasonably good condition inside, just some scattered light spotting and, of course, darkened end-papers. As she carefully flipped through a few pages, an envelope fell out and onto the floor. It was addressed to Grace's flat in England. Inside was a doctor's report with her name on it, the date was one week after her birth.

'Our findings are that significant, possibly irreversible nerve damage has occurred to the patient's right shoulder. The injury seems to have been caused by the infant falling and by the mother, while attempting rescue, inadvertently stretched the shoulder, severely injuring the brachial plexus.'

Wait a minute, she thought, *I was told my arm was injured during birth. This has to be wrong.* There was also an attached letter.

Dear Grace,

I'm sorry I didn't listen to you all those years. I know now what your sister is capable of and am fearing for my own life. I believe your sister and Keaton are trying to kill me, and I need your help. I've always known Mervin caused the injury to your arm when you were just a week old. I lied to the doctors and to the family to protect her. Even your father didn't know the truth until years later. She always had it in for you from the beginning. I guess it was jealousy after being the only child for ten years. I am so sorry about lying to you and never helping you. I don't know why I always protected your sister. I hope you can forgive a stupid old woman and come to her rescue now. There's so much you need to know. I'm frightened, Grace.

I love you.

Mother

The letter was shaking in Grace's hands. In fact, her entire body was shaking uncontrollably. She had no idea what to do with this information. She looked around the room blankly, shaking her head in disbelief. Grace jumped as the cell phone rang, bringing her out of her stupor.

"Hello?" Grace's voice was faint and crackly.

"Grace? You sound weird. Are you okay?" It was Cameron.

"Um, I'm fine," Grace lied. "Just dealing with something at the moment. Things are really messed up around here."

"I've had a bad feeling lately, been worried about you. Why don't you come over? Get away from that house."

Grace could use someone to talk to after finding this devastating discovery, and getting away from here sounded like a great idea.

"Perfect timing, actually, Cameron. I could use a shoulder." Grace smoothed her hair behind her ears.

"Great. Come anytime. I'll cook us a nice meal. Do us a wee favor lass and keep an eye out for Piper on your way over, will ye? I haven't seen him since early this morning. I've just come back from calling him but no sign. Ach, he's probably oot messing wi' them rabbits again." He gave a slight chuckle, but Grace could hear that he was getting worried.

"I absolutely will. I'm sure Piper will show up soon, though. See you soon, Cameron, and thank you."

As Grace hung up, she noticed something strange on the bedroom wall opposite her bed. It was a hole the size of a coin.

She tried to peek inside it but saw only blackness. She went into the adjoining guest room. The hole was directly located in the guest room's closet. When she opened the closet door, her mouth nearly hit the floor. Inside was a blanket, a pillow, and a glass of water covered with plastic film wrap. Her missing cell phone was in there as well.

Someone's been watching me. In my room! She felt sick to her stomach, her mind was reeling. Her whole life was built on lies and deceit. She had to get the hell out of this madhouse!

Grace grabbed her suitcase and began packing. There had to be a 'Bed and Breakfast' nearby. She'd had enough of this asylum.

She wanted to confront Morvin about everything, but there was so much going on. She couldn't wrap her head around it all. Morvin had possibly poisoned her mother and aunt, her mother was afraid for her life, and her disability was caused by her sister. On top of all that, someone's been secretly watching her!

She'd go talk to Cameron and tell him everything that was going on. She realized she'd really just met the man but he seemed nice, decent...kind. Grace had to trust someone, she needed help with all of this.

Grace changed into her black dress pants and put on a pretty, light blouse. She washed her face, put on some makeup, and put up her hair. She checked herself in the mirror before heading out and thought she looked nice enough, presentable for sure. Was that enough? Should she put on something sexier? She was definitely attracted to Cameron. He had that adorable accent and a pretty great body too... *Oh my god, Grace. Really? With everything that's happening, you're actually hot and bothered for some man you barely know? Get a grip, woman.*

She grabbed her bags and headed out the door but paused briefly in the hall. She went back to the mirror, let her hair down and tousled it a bit.

CHAPTER TWENTY-EIGHT

"**P**ASS IT OVER, man."

"Okay, okay," said Keaton. "Hold your gob a minute."

Keaton and his two friends were out driving around the town. They had been at an outdoor party most of the afternoon, but it had become windy and started raining. Most of the people left, and the party got boring. Empty booze bottles rolled and clashed together on the car floor as they raced through the wet country streets.

"Pass it over," insisted Matthew, who was Keaton's oldest friend and possessed even less ambition. He had to practically yell over the blasting metal rock on the stereo, so he reached in front of Keaton's face and ripped the joint out of his fingers. The hot ember landed on Keaton's lap, and he started jumping all over the front seat. The driver,

Gavin, laughed hysterically. He swerved the car and drove onto the shoulder. Beyond the shoulder was a long drop to the fast-flowing Blackmore River.

They were fast approaching Cotter's Bridge when they were jostled by an ugly bump under the 2003 Honda Accord.

Gavin stopped the car. "What was that?" he asked his intoxicated mates.

"I don't know. Who cares? Probably just a badger or something. Let's go." Keaton batted out the ember on his crotch and was still giggling about it.

Gavin got out and walked to the back of the car. He came running back to the passenger side, and as he swung open the door, Keaton fell out and onto the ground. Matthew, in the backseat, was beside himself with laughter. He got out and pointed down at Keaton, howling, and holding his stomach.

Gavin wasn't laughing. "We fuckin' hit someone! We hit some guy. Get over here."

Keaton and Matthew looked at each other quizzically, their laughter subsiding. They flipped their hoods over their heads to shield the rain and followed.

"Holy shit," said Keaton. Behind the car, a man lay bleeding and moaning. His moans came out in a gurgle as his mouth was full of blood. Keaton looked closer at the man's face. "Hey, I know this guy. He came snooping around the house the other day, looking for my aunt."

"Look at his leg, man," said Gavin. "Gross."

"Oh, sick," Keaton said. The man's leg was severely twisted the wrong way, and there was bone protruding through his ripped pants around the knee area. Matthew wasn't saying anything. He stood there with his hand over his mouth, eyes wide. Gavin checked for damage to his mum's car.

"Can't see much damage on the car. What do we do? What are you looking for, Keats?"

Keaton was scanning the sodden ground. He walked over to the edge of the road and picked up a sizable boulder with both hands. He held it up over his head, and, just before bringing it down hard, he said, "I can't get caught with this shit. I'll be seriously buggered. So will you guys." He slammed the rock down on the wounded man's head with all his strength. There was a loud crack and a wet, sickening crunch. The man was still gurgling lightly.

"What the fuck are you doing, Keaton? We can call the cops and then just take off. They'll never know who did it." Gavin said. Matthew went back inside the car.

"No way, man. I'm not risking jail time for this piece of shit. Look at him, he was gonna die anyway." Keaton lifted the boulder and brought it down hard again on the dying man's skull. This one finished the job.

Keaton noticed a paper bag a few feet from where the man lay. He picked it up and pulled out a bottle of wine. Keaton unscrewed the cap and took a long swig. "Oh crap, poor taste in wine too, heh, heh." He took one more big swallow and poured the rest on the man's chest, then threw the bottle on the dead body. It bounced off his stomach and rolled away.

Keaton checked the man's pockets and found a wallet. "Marcus James Foster," he opened the billfold. "Woohoo, look at this. There's gotta be at least two hundred pounds here. Let's go party, man."

"You are seriously deranged. Give me that," Gavin snatched the ID out of Keaton's hand. "What kind of name is Marcus anyway? Sounds like a faggot."

"Help me get him over to the edge before a car comes," said Keaton. He yelled over to Matthew. "Get over here, you pansy-ass and help."

They could hear Matthew puking into the dirt by the car and started laughing. "I guess it's up to us, Gav."

They dragged the body by the arms to the edge of the cliff and rolled it over, sending it plunging down into the wet fogginess some hundred feet below. They were worried for a second as it looked like the body was going to stay on the bank. But gravity and momentum carried it successfully into the rapids and down the river.

"Did you see him go?" asked Gavin. "I can't see nothin'."

"Well, I definitely heard a splash. Yeah, yeah, he's gone," Keaton gave a mock salute. "Bon voyage, Marcus, you faggot." The two young men had a good laugh at that and then walked back to the car. "Hey Matt, you pussy. Thanks a lot for your help." He threw the ID card at him. "Get rid of this ASAP. At least you can do that much."

They got back in the car, and Gavin peeled out on the gravel, sending dirt and rocks flying out behind the tires.

CHAPTER TWENTY-NINE

S HE HAD HER hand on the doorknob, ready to turn it and get the hell out of this nightmare.

"You're leaving us?" Morvin asked, with a nasty smirk on her haggard face. Grace could barely see her looming silhouette through the darkness of the gloomy foyer.

Grace was ready to pounce, rage boiling just under the surface, ready to explode on her sister. *Don't lose it, Grace,* she told herself. "As a matter of fact, I am. I've had about all I can take of this house."

"Oh?" Morvin sneered. "Keaton will be so disappointed that you're heading back home so soon, as am I." She was holding a teacup and saucer, stirring while she spoke. "I'll have Piers contact you there when the papers are ready for you to sign." She walked toward Grace, her small black heels clicking on the wood floor. "I am glad to see that you've come to your senses and realized that you don't have any right to the inheritance. It was me that cared for Mother all these years, after all." She was shaking her head at Grace, looking at her like she was stupid and useless, the way she always had, always did. She sipped her tea through her thin, wrinkled lips.

Grace couldn't take it, enough was enough. "Oh, I'm not leaving Scotland," Grace smiled. "Not until I see to it that not only do you and your sick bastard of a son get nothing, but I'm going to make sure you pay." Grace leaned into Morvin's face, her teeth gritted and neck straining. "Pay for everything you've done. I read one of those letters from Mother. You remember, the ones you hid from me? She was afraid for her life. She knew you were trying to kill her. You will not get away with this, Morvin."

"Oh, my God. Poor gimpy Grace," Morvin scoffed. "I know you may think you're onto something, stupid girl, but you know nothing. Mother was very loopy near the end. She was doing some pretty crazy things, putting fake flowers in water, getting simple words wrong. She actually even forgot I had a sister! Can you imagine? It's all been documented by my doctor." She turned her back to Grace and began walking away. "Now, run along," she said with a wave of her hand, "and take that pathetic, hideous, gimpy hand with you. It's been making me sick to have to see that thing every day."

That was it. Grace caught up behind Morvin, whirled her around by her arm and slapped her hard, right across the face. The cup and saucer smashed to the floor as Morvin gasped and put her hand to the reddening welt.

"You can't hurt me anymore," Grace said calmly,

smiling. "Your words *don't* hurt me anymore at all. You're the pathetic one. You're going to die a lonely, sad old woman after I'm through with proving everything you've done to this family. Goodbye, Morvin."

Grace turned around, grabbed her bags, and slammed the door behind her. "Now whose smirking, you vile old bat? Wow...that felt *great!*"

CHAPTER THIRTY

I T WAS STARTING to sprinkle again as Grace put her bags in the car. She got in behind the wheel and then quickly slumped down as a car sped up the driveway. Keaton got out of the passenger side, along with a few beer cans and fast-food wrappers. He yelled something incoherent to the driver and staggered to Morvin's car. He fell into the driver's seat and peeled off, following the other vehicle back down the driveway.

"Lovely boy you've got there, Morvin," Grace said to herself.

She decided to walk to Cameron's, taking the back way through the property, thinking that with Keaton gone, this would be a perfect opportunity to explore his domain. There was bound to be something significant there to prove both Morvin and Keaton's guilt.

A fine mist coated her face as she made her way through the light fog to the outbuildings area. Keaton's dwelling appeared faintly in the distance, getting clearer as she got closer. The fog thickened suddenly and was now like gray, cold, damp cotton.

The foliage around the building was overgrown, like the rest of the property. Grace took a quick look behind her as she ascended the creaky wood stairs and tried the door. Locked. She squinted through the large window beside the door, but it was impossible to see clearly through the years of built-up grime and dirt.

Grace walked around the left side of the small building, recalling that this particular one used to be Wilson's living quarters. Grace remembered playing here, being quite a pest to the friendly groundskeeper, but he never complained or scolded her.

She tried the back door, also locked. Grace thought about trying a window when she noticed a small shed at the back of the little yard. This was padlocked, but it was so brittle she managed, with a bit of effort, to push it open, breaking the old rusted metal hasp. The smell hit her immediately like a punch in the stomach. As she covered her nose with the collar of her sweater, flies swarmed in front of her face. What was that smell? It was earthy, rotting, and sickeningly sweet.

She made her way carefully to the back of the shed, stepping over tools, and old gardening supplies. It was very dark, with not much light coming in on this wet, misty morning; with the dirty windows, not much could anyway.

Grace froze when she suddenly heard a twig snap.

Someone was coming. She found a dark corner and backed into it, knocking over an old tin watering can in the process. She cringed as it crashed loudly to the floor and pressed herself into the shadow of the wall. The footsteps were coming closer, no doubt to investigate the noise. *Maybe he'll think it was a squirrel and walk away. Damn, he's going to notice the lock is broken.*

After her confrontation with Keaton in her mother's room and the way he leered at her the other day, Grace knew this young man was seriously unstable and troubled. Who knows what he'd do if he caught her snooping around his house.

She heard him enter the shed. She could hear herself breathing and was sure he could as well. Grace closed her eyes, praying for invisibility, trying to stay absolutely still. She held her breath. *Please go away, please, turn around and go away.* His feet shuffled in the dirt of the doorway. Was he coming further in? She had to breathe, had to take a breath. As she opened her mouth to inhale the putrid air, she heard her own spittle make a noise as her lips parted.

More shuffling noises, more steps. The steps sounded to be getting farther away. He was leaving, but Grace dared not move. At least she could breathe and open her eyes, but she was not moving until it felt safe enough to do so. What if he was watching the shed? How would she get out of here?

Movement in front of the outbuilding caught Grace's eye as a large hooded man appeared outside. He lifted his gaze in her direction. The man took off his hood and peered through the window. Grace had to stifle a gasp when she saw the familiar large scar down the right side of his face. He backed up, replaced his hood, and headed toward the main house.

She finally took a breath and allowed herself to come out of the shadows. As she made her way to the doorway, she stubbed her toe on a 2x4 plank, and it sent her hurtling forward, almost bashing her face on a shelf. As she righted herself, she discovered the source of the smell. She was face to face with the severed head of a dog.

She couldn't tell if it was Piper or not, but this had obviously been here for a while. She almost tripped over her own feet in her haste to get the hell away from the corpse.

Grace ran for the trail that led to the back of the estate and to Cameron's. She stopped short, though, when she heard a faint crying noise. She waited. There it was again. A definite whining followed by scratching. It was coming from somewhere to her right, in the trees. She followed the sound.

The sound got louder, and she saw a large cage behind a cluster of spruce trees. Inside the cage was Piper, tied tight by the neck to one side and muzzled. The cage door was padlocked.

"It's okay, Piper. I'll get you out," said Grace. The poor dog looked at her with sad, pleading eyes. He was so excited to see her that he was nearly strangling himself. "Calm down, buddy, it's okay."

She searched the ground for a rock, keeping an eye on her surroundings for the hooded psychopath or Keaton. A few feet away, she found a sharp-edged rock and, after a few tries, managed to smash the lock open. Poor Piper was coughing and gagging now from the tight rope around his neck. Grace finally freed him after struggling with the knot, and Piper's large flailing body, and then removed the muzzle from his face. He knocked Grace over with kisses as soon as his mouth was free.

"Come on, boy," said Grace. "Let's get you home."

CHAPTER THIRTY-ONE

"I'M GOING TO tear that little bastard apart!" The veins were bulging out of Cameron's neck. He'd checked Piper over, and the dog seemed fine, just incredibly thirsty.

"I know, and I don't blame you. But please, Cameron, I need to get all of this straight in my head first. I want to go about this the right way so that they fry for everything they've done." Grace led him to a kitchen chair and motioned for him to sit.

"Well, you're not going back into that house. That's for bloody sure."

"I agree. I'm seriously scared," Grace confided. "It all points to Morvin." Grace began pacing while she talked. "I believe she poisoned my mum because Keaton is in huge financial trouble, and, let's face it, the house is falling apart. Morvin needed money, and my poor mother was standing in the way of her getting it." She stopped pacing and looked at him. "And I think she did it with the water hemlock plant. I found a book in my father's library about it. Apparently, ingesting it can cause cardiac arrest."

Cameron got up from the table and poured them each a glass of wine.

"Cameron, I found a plant, which looks a lot like water hemlock, in Morvin's garden." Grace took a big swallow.

"But you don't seriously think your sister is capable of actual murder, do you?" Cameron asked.

"Well, I know she's a very jealous, miserable old crone who'd do anything for that waste of oxygen she calls a son." Grace held out her empty glass for a refill. "Let's not forget that poisonous gas order Charlie called about. I looked into that too and, if inhaled, it can cause stroke-like symptoms. What if Aunt Lena was on her way to talk to me, but Morvin got to her first?" Grace sat back down. "I'm going to the police with all this first thing tomorrow morning, Cameron. Will you come with me? And," Grace paused and looked at her glass, "is it okay if I stay the night?"

"Absolutely. That's a good idea," Cameron said. "But this is all just too incredible. I mean, we're not living in one of my novels. This stuff only happens in the movies, right?"

Grace put her head in her hands and fought back the tears. *He's going to think my family and I are a bunch of nutcases,* she thought.

He went over and rubbed her shoulders. Then he gently turned her to face him. "I'm with you on this, Grace. We'll see it through together in the morning. For now, I want you to try and relax. You're safe here." He took her chin in his big hand and kissed her gently on the lips. He moved her hair off her forehead and smiled at her, looking into her eyes, saying nothing, not having to.

"Thank you, Cameron," she leaned forward and gave him a kiss this time. She parted his lips with her tongue, and he welcomed it. The kiss deepened, their breath quickened. She felt her insides pleasantly begin to quiver and knew if she didn't back off now, there would soon be a point of no return. She wasn't ready for that. She eased off.

"Wow," she whispered. "Sorry about that. I'm having some trouble controlling myself around you."

"Don't hold back on my account," he said, smiling. "I should take a look at my sauce. I hope you like spaghetti. It's one of my specialties."

"It smells amazing, Cameron."

They continued to talk in detail about Grace's situation over more wine and a delicious dinner. Grace told him about the unopened letters she found in Morvin's bedroom. She told him about all the lies and about her disability.

"I hadn't noticed your arm. You do very well we' it," he said.

They moved to the couch in the sitting room, bringing their wine with them.

Cameron lit a small fire and then sat down close beside Grace. He put his arm around her shoulders. She felt worlds away from Craigrook. It felt incredible...he was incredible.

Piper joined them in the sitting room and let out an audible sigh as he laid down in his bed by the hearth.

"That was some truly amazing spaghetti, Cameron. You sure you're not Italian?" she asked, grinning.

"Maybe somewhere down the bloodlines, eh? I'm glad you liked it. Wait until you try one of my killer steaks."

"I love a man who knows his way around a kitchen." She changed position and kneeled beside him, one arm leaning on the back of the settee.

He squinted his eyes and looked at her quizzically. "You can't cook, can you?"

"Not even toast," she said and laughed loudly. Cameron laughed too.

"Come here, hen," he said then, looking serious. "I want to kiss you again."

Once again, the kiss started out soft and gentle but then quickly gained heat. Grace felt that quivering sensation deep within her and suddenly wanted him urgently, no stopping things this time.

Cameron's strong hands explored her body through her clothes, but soon, that wasn't enough, and he began to pull up her blouse. Grace suddenly backed away from him.

"I'm sorry, love," he whispered gently. "Am I going too fast?"

She wanted him badly. Being with him felt so right. "No, not at all. I just—" She took a deep breath and pulled her blouse over her head. She turned her back to him. "It's just these scars. I'm worried you'll find them ugly and change your mind about being with me."

He said nothing for a few seconds, and she was about to put her clothes back on when she felt him start to gently kiss her back. Tears welled up in her eyes as he continued to kiss and caress every single scar.

She turned to him then, and in unison, he laid on top of her as she lay on her back. He undid her jeans, and she wriggled out of them. He sat up straight, and she saw his taut, chest muscles as he stretched out of his t-shirt and threw it on the floor behind him. *My god, he is the sexiest man alive.*

He kissed down her neck, her stomach, slowly, taking his time, exploring her. She arched her back as he tasted every inch of her. He stood then and took off his jeans. He had a gorgeous body, naturally muscular, with light hair in all the right places.

He laid his body lightly on her again and looked deeply, knowingly, into her eyes. Then gently but powerfully, took her. She wrapped her legs around his waist, allowing him every inch of her, the pleasure made her moan loudly and arch her neck in ecstasy.

He leaned down and grabbed the back of her neck, pulled her face to his, and kissed her. "You are so bloody beautiful," he whispered.

She exploded then, in an intense rush of heated, glorious passion, and he followed.

They laid there together, in each other's arms, in silence for a time, as their breathing slowed to normal. Cameron brushed her temples lightly with his fingertips.

"It's okay if you want to ask," she said softly.

"If you want to tell me, I'm listening," he responded.

"Morvin was very cruel to me when I was growing up. These scars are from just one of the times she physically hurt me."

"Look, Grace. There's a fawn down there," Morvin said, excitement in her voice.

"No, there isn't. I don't believe you," said Grace. Grace would love to see a fawn, though, and was tempted to look out over the hill.

"I'm not lying. You're going to miss it. It's so cute," lured Morvin, knowing her sister's pathetic love of all animals.

She couldn't help herself. Maybe Morvin was telling the truth; she could be kind sometimes. Just enough so that she could suck Grace in when she wanted to.

Grace went over to the edge of the cliff and looked down below. She could see thick prickly brambles, all dried out from the summer months. The slope was steep and full of sticks and broken branches from the trees above. She couldn't see any deer down there.

"It's right there. Are you blind as well as useless? Look, there's its mother," Morvin said.

"Where, where?" Grace asked, eager to see the mother deer.

Morvin pushed Grace's back, and she started to fall forward. Morvin grabbed Grace's left arm by the wrist. Grace lost her foothold and screamed.

"Oops," said Morvin. "What are you going to do now, stupid?"

"Help me, Morvin, I'm going to fall. *Please help me!*" Grace was crying, squealing with fear.

"Come on, Grace. All you have to do to save yourself is reach out with your right hand, and I'll grab it."

Grace tried to move her right arm up to Morvin's

outstretched hand, but her arm didn't work like that. The destroyed nerves, caused by physical trauma as an infant, drastically reduced most movement.

"I can't."

"Aww, what's that? You can't? Poor gimpy Grace, such a sad waste of space," she chided. "Oh well, goodbye." And with that final word, she let go of Grace's wrist, sending her rolling down the steep, gnarly hill. She watched with perverse delight as her sister screamed, rolling, rolling, branches and sharp twigs snapping under her little body, or were those bones breaking? Morvin giggled to herself.

Grace felt hard sticks poking into her skin, through her clothes, all over her body. As she was falling, it was like her mind blocked out the pain until she finally came to a stop at the bottom. All around her were prickly brambles. Then the pain came all at once, and it was excruciating. She screamed in agony as she struggled to gain some footing and get out of the tangles. Her panic only entangled her further and the needles and prickles wedged deeper into her skin.

"What's happened?" Grace heard her daddy's voice from above.

"Help!" Grace squealed. "Daddy!"

"She fell. Help her, Father. She fell down the hill. I didn't know what to do!" Morvin pleaded.

The big man held on to a long, overhanging tree branch and made his way slowly down the steep hill. At the bottom, he managed to stand on a large rock, then he bent over and scooped Grace out of the prickly brush.

Grace was covered in blood. He quickly got her back up the hill and raced across the field to his car with Morvin right on his heels. Grace cried in agony as he drove her to the nearby doctor.

"Okay, Gracey," said Dr. Solder, "just a couple more to go." He tied off the last stitch and covered it with a bandage. Grace winced at the sting. "That's it. Thank goodness nothing was broken. What a tumble, my dear. What happened?"

Grace looked over through tears at Morvin. She wanted to tell them Morvin had pushed her. Morvin was standing behind her father. She made a motion with her hands, imitating snapping Grace's cat's neck, which was Morvin's favorite tactic to stop Grace from telling.

Grace had found a stray white cat a few months before. She fell in love with the little blue-eyed kitten instantly and pleaded to keep her. She named the cat Casper after her favorite cartoon about the friendly ghost. Morvin would often kick the cat out of the way or dangle it from the foyer stairs to torment little Grace. She even changed the words to the cartoon theme song. Grace would start crying every time Morvin sang it: 'Casper, the bleeding cat. The bloodiest cat you know.' Grace knew, all too well, what this motion of Morvin's hands meant.

As Grace tried to decide what to say, Morvin started humming the cartoon theme song, as she pretended to be interested in a magazine.

"I just slipped and fell," Grace said, the tears streaming down her dirty face. Dr. Solder handed Grace a red sucker and lifted her off the examination bed. Her body hurt all over.

"You be more careful, sweetheart," he said. "She'll be

fine, Wallace," he said to Grace's father, "just see that she takes it easy for a few days and keep the wounds clean. We'll remove the stitches in a few weeks." He handed Morvin a sucker too. "Must have got a fright there, eh, Morvin? You're not too old for suckers, are you?"

"Not at all, Dr. Solder, thank you. It was just horrible." She gave Grace a grin and a wink as they headed out the office door.

CHAPTER THIRTY-TWO

CAMERON WOKE UP alarmed by Piper's barking. He looked around the room and saw Grace lying beside him. He laid back down and smiled, remembering the incredible night before.

They'd both fallen asleep in the sitting room. Cameron woke up in the middle of the night with a sore neck. He tried to rouse Grace, but she just moaned and rolled over, so he picked her up and carried her to his bed. As he laid her down, he heard her giggle.

"Cheeky wee bugger," he said.

They'd made love again, slower this time, and then fallen back to sleep, sated and spent. He watched her while she slept. He barely knew this woman, yet he was always thinking about her. He was drawn to her and grew more fond of her by the minute.

The loss of his wife Meg had been brutal. They'd fought her cancer hard for three long years only to have it seat itself finally in her pancreas and then finish her off in three short months.

There is not a more hopeless feeling than watching your partner, your best friend, suffer in so much pain. Seeing them wither away until there is nothing left, and there is absolutely nothing you can do to help her, to save her is the worst pain.

After she passed, he poured himself into his writing. He didn't see their friends anymore. He couldn't look at their piteous expressions or listen to endless suggestions about how he needed to get on. He knew they meant well, but got tired of saying no to their ceaseless invitations to dinners and parties, so he cut himself off entirely. He had no desire for company, other than Piper, for so long...until now. Until Grace walked, or rather jogged, into his life. He didn't even realize how lonely he was. Maybe he could build a life with someone again, something he believed impossible only days ago.

He moved a strand of dark curls off her face and touched her cheek. She was sleeping so soundly. He leaned over and softly kissed her forehead.

I won't let anyone hurt you, my sweet Grace, he thought, as he began to drift back to sleep. In the living room, though, Piper started barking again. Fiercely this time, growling and snorting.

"What the hell's up wi' him?" Cameron muttered quietly as he got out of bed. He hopped into a pair of jeans, shoved on his slippers, and went to check it out.

"What's going on, buddy?" he asked, as the dog

continued barking at the front door. "Okay, okay. Let's go see what's got you all flustered."

Cameron pulled on a t-shirt as he opened the door. Piper beelined it across the side yard, and then through the grove of fir trees that flanked the stables. In the pre-dawn light, the dark woods seemed to swallow the dog whole.

He felt the chill of the fall morning as he tried to catch up to Piper. Cameron worried about his dog after what that maniac Keaton had done to him.

On the other side of the trees, there was an old, abandoned, stable building that was roughly fifty yards south of the main cottage. Cameron had only been in it once since he began renting the place six or seven years ago. It had lain empty and unused except for the storage of some old potato crates and discarded furniture odds and ends.

"Piper! Piper!" Cameron called. *Silly animal, probably after another bloody rabbit.* Still, it was a strange way for him to act. He was usually a very placid dog. He followed the sound of Piper's incessant barking through the woods to the old stone and wood stable building. Twigs and stones poked the bottom of his feet; slippers were not the best choice for this terrain.

He walked around to the back and turned sharply as Piper's barking turned vicious. It sounded like he was in a fight. Now Cameron was running.

"Piper!" The wide, sliding barn door stood open. "Piper!" The dog must have gone inside. As soon as Cameron entered the building, everything went black as he was hit in the head from behind.

He detected the faint smell of smoke just before he went down.

CHAPTER THIRTY-THREE

A SUDDEN NOISE WOKE her, and she looked around the room, confused. A slow grin spread across Grace's face as memories of the night before came back, and she remembered where she was. She felt rested after a much-needed, deep sleep. Must have been the feeling of safety, his strong arms around her all night. She glanced beside her. *Where is he?* She wrapped herself in a blanket and headed to the kitchen to find him.

"Cameron?" she called out. "Hmm, not here." *Maybe he took Piper out,* she thought.

She went into the sitting room, and absentmindedly started biting her nails as she looked at the couch and thought about the events of the evening before. She hugged herself and swooned, the silly grin still on her face. *Cameron is so awesome, he's perfect. Oh my God,* she thought, *I think I'm in love with him.*

Grace drew the sheers apart at the front window to see if she could see him in the yard. She noticed a handwritten note on the floor in front of the door.

Grace,

Please come to the house immediately. I've done some hard thinking since you left and I need to talk, I need to confess. You were absolutely right to be angry, I'm so sorry about everything, but there are things you don't understand, things I can explain. Please come quickly. I'm afraid I may hurt myself. I need you.

Love, Morvin

Grace had never heard Morvin sound so needy and apologetic. She seemed so desperate in the letter. Grace had told Cameron she wouldn't go back to the house by herself, but her sister might be ready to get the help she needed. Where was he anyway?

Grace put the blanket on the bed and quickly got dressed. Maybe she'd just talk to her through the door. *Yes, that'd be fine,* Grace told herself. *I won't go in the house. And besides, I've got the cell phone if anything happens.*

She ran into the den and grabbed a pencil from Cameron's desk. She turned Morvin's note over and wrote one for Cameron on the back.

Grace was out of breath when she reached the front steps of Craigrook. On the way over, she'd begun to worry about what Morvin said about hurting herself. If her sister could truthfully explain all the events that had transpired, then maybe there was a way to help her. She couldn't take another death in the family. Morvin was the only one left...well, besides Keaton, but he seemed to be beyond help, really.

She ran up the steps and found the front door open. *Why would that be? It's freezing outside.*

"Morvin?" Grace called out from the doorway, not entirely entering the house as she'd promised. "Morvin!" she yelled a little louder.

She heard a faint voice answer, but it sounded weak and far away. She entered the foyer, listening closer. "Morvin?"

Again the faint voice, only now it sounded like it was coming from upstairs. What if Morvin had done something drastic? What if she needed Grace's immediate help?

Grace ascended the stairs warily. "Morvin? Is that you?"

"Yes," said Morvin. "Hurry, come up here. Quickly, Grace."

She still sounded weak, but it was definitely Morvin. "Where are you?" Grace asked.

"On the terrace. I need to see you."

The terrace? She didn't think anyone went up there anymore. It was a rooftop terrace that her family enjoyed long ago. Her parents often threw parties up there when Grace was young. But after Father disappeared, the parties stopped, and no one bothered with it. It became weathered, the floor soft in spots, dangerous to walk on.

The entrance to the terrace was on the uppermost floor of the house, to be entered by a skinny staircase from one of the attic rooms.

"Hurry, Grace. Hurry up!" said Morvin, distressed,

her voice coming in clearer now as Grace climbed the four flights and reached the attic floor.

There were three attic rooms at Craigrook. Two were used mainly for storage, and the larger one was used as a gathering space. If it got too chilly on the terrace, guests could come inside and still enjoy drinks and music away from the often cool Scottish evenings.

The room hadn't changed at all, much like the rest of the house. It was an eerie, dusty relic, and it gave Grace goosebumps. The record player still sat in the far corner, where the harmonic notes of Montovani played into the night. The room smelled of too much time passing without a stir to move the staleness. She remembered the busy sounds of glasses clinking and the laughter of the many guests. It was all still so vivid in her mind but now sadly gone forever.

She remembered being shooed away by her father, the smell of scotch on his breath, "Bed now Gracey, too late for little girls." But Grace would linger on the stairs for a bit longer, enjoying the happy, festive sounds from beyond the door.

Grace walked to the thin, tall door that led to the staircase and, ultimately, to the roof. She carefully made her way up the fifteen, very steep, creaky, dark steps to the top. Grace pushed open the door.

How could have been so stupid, so gullible? Fear surged through her body as she found herself looking straight into the pointed edge of a large, gleaming butcher knife. At the other end was a sneering, grinning Morvin.

CHAPTER THIRTY-FOUR

THE OLD BUILDING was perfect kindling, and the fire was eating it up. Even the dampness of the season couldn't slow down the steady burn of the aging structure.

Piper knew his master was in danger inside the smoke-filled building. He continuously barked at the large door and jumped at the side window, clearing over four feet with every spring. His nails scratched the glass, but he couldn't gather enough force to break it.

Cameron lay on the sawdust floor inside the burning building. He could faintly hear barking coming from somewhere, but full consciousness remained under a thick film of fog.

He was back in the hospital with his wife, Meg. She was alive and improving. Their prayers had been answered, and they were smiling at each other, holding hands. Neither was speaking, just staring into each other's eyes.

Someone came through the door. It was Grace. She looked radiant, dressed in a light floral frock, her brown curly hair bouncing about her shoulders. Cameron stood and went to her and kissed her passionately on the lips. They were laughing. Then he remembered Meg was lying in the hospital bed, watching them. He went to her side, she was crying, shaking her head in disbelief.

"How could you, Cameron? Why?" she kept asking, over and over.

But he had no explanation, he had nothing to say. He couldn't understand it himself. As Meg cried, her face grew thinner by the second. Her skin turned gray and gaunt. Cameron held her hand and pleaded, "No!" He was losing her again, and he couldn't stop it.

Meg's face was skeletal now, and her hand was skin and bone in his. He watched in absolute horror as the skin on her face began to rot and fall away, bone revealed underneath. Her hair fell out onto the pillow, and her body melted and withered in front of his eyes.

He looked over at Grace. Terror struck him as he saw that she was engulfed in flames. She was still standing, but her entire form was on fire. He stood and went close to her, but the heat was unbearable, he couldn't save her either. He fell to the ground as the whole hospital room began burning. He struggled to breathe through the smoke.

Cameron lay unconscious in the barn, stuck in his horrific nightmare. Flames continued to grow, smoke now billowing out of the walls and under the door. The fire had already spread halfway across the roof, eating away at the support beams above Cameron's head. With a loud crack, one of them gave way, crashing down only a foot from his leg. The noise jolted him, bringing him somewhat to his senses. He opened his eyes and coughed as he looked around him and gradually realized his situation. He tried to stand and stumbled, as stabbing pain seized his head. Cameron staggered to the door and pushed, but it was blocked from the outside, where Piper barked frantically.

"Okay...okay boy. I hear you," Cameron wheezed.

The smoke strangled him. His lungs scalded with each searing, toxic inhale. He looked up as another booming crack threatened; the whole roof could come down at any time.

Cameron saw a shovel lying on the barn floor. It had blood on one end...probably his. He wound up and smashed the shovel on the window, breaking the glass. The sudden burst of oxygen fed the flames, and the fire now fully engulfed the roof.

The window was too high for Cameron to reach without something to stand on. There were stacks of potato crates on the far wall, but they were already consumed by fire. He only needed something a half a foot high; he could pull himself up the rest of the way. Cameron shielded his face as the roof at the far end of the barn gave way, sending smoke and huge burning embers directly at him. He had to get out now.

Cameron grabbed the shovel and leaned it against the wall under the window, he stood on the footrest and tried to get a hold of the ledge. Sharp glass stabbed through his fingers. He lost his balance, and the shovel fell over. He landed hard on his back, and consciousness once more began to elude him. Cameron thought of Grace, the danger she was in. He had to get out of here so he could protect her, save her like he couldn't do for Meg. He fought the haze that permeated his brain, but he was so exhausted, so fatigued.

He rolled over, coughing and gagging from the intense smoke and heat. Outside Piper continued barking and jumping at the window.

His dog needed him too. Piper would never give up on Cameron, so he forced himself to keep moving.

He leaned the shovel against the wall again, but this time he jabbed the point of it into the sawdust floor to brace it. Cameron put both feet on the footrest and tried to ignore the pain from the window glass and the burning torch in his lungs. He pulled himself up until he could get his elbow on the ledge. Glass pierced deep into his skin. He heaved with all his might and managed to get enough of his body out of the opening. Gravity did the rest, and Cameron fell out the window headfirst into a pile of glass shards that stabbed into his scalp and back.

Piper began licking his face, his paws bloody as well from repeatedly jumping on the broken glass. Cameron staggered to his feet, and the two ran away from the burning building, which was now completely engulfed.

They had almost reached the main cottage when the entire building collapsed behind them, huge flames lit up the whole property.

Cameron ran into the cottage. "Grace! Grace!" he yelled through fits of coughing, he ran from room to room. "Where is she, Piper?" He noticed a note on the table. He couldn't believe it. "She didn't really go up there...alone?"

Panicked, he headed out the door for Craigrook House, praying he wasn't too late.

CHAPTER THIRTY-FIVE

"WHAT ARE YOU doing, Morvin?" Grace said, shaking all over. "Put the knife down. We'll get you the help you need. You don't have to do this."

"You're the one that needs help, Grace. Back up. *Move!*" Morvin's eyes darted everywhere, her pupils so big they almost covered the white, giving her a possessed look. Her lips were curled into a snarling grimace.

Grace glanced around her at the dilapidated terrace. It used to be such a magical place, all lit up with twinkle lights and adorned with gorgeous flowers from end to end. But now it was bare, dirty, and neglected. A strong wind blew dust, leaves, and debris into swirling mini-tornadoes. There were puddles of water where the roof was warped and soft from years of battering rain and heavy snowfall.

"What's wrong with you? Why have you done these

things to our family? To our own mother?" Grace continued to be led backward, the knife right in front of her nose. "Now you're going to kill me too? Cameron, the man that's staying in the Gittens' cottage? He knows everything. You're still going to jail even if I'm dead."

Morvin closed her eyes tight and shook her head back and forth. "Shut up, shut up, *shut up!* You really are such a pain in my ass. You always have been." The wind was really picking up now, whipping Morvin's hair around her face. It was getting in her eyes and stuck in her twisted mouth, but she didn't care. She seemed oblivious to it.

"Why did you do it, Morvin? How could you kill our mother?" Grace asked.

A maniacal grin spread across Morvin's face. "I didn't kill your mother, you stupid little tart. I killed your grandmother." She threw her head back and laughed.

"What are you talking about?" This made no sense. Morvin had really lost it. She had Grace backed up against the terrace railing. Grace looked nervously down at the ground, at least six stories below.

Rain began falling hard, it stung Grace's face, cold and cutting. "You killed them for money, didn't you, Morvin? Because Keaton is in real trouble. I understand that. You'd do anything to protect your son." Grace said, trying to reason with her, talk her down. "Anyone would do the same thing for their child."

Morvin's face turned sour, "Yes, I did it. I killed them all. Mother was being selfish with her money, and then Lena was a busybody about everything. Should've minded her own business, that one. And so should you!" She held the sharp knife against Grace's cheek. Grace could feel a trickle of warm blood run down her face.

"Father was the first one, though," Morvin continued with a straight, sober face, as though she was talking about a grocery list instead of a kill list. She heard Grace gasp. She liked it. "He had to go. He wanted to send me away. He wanted to tell everyone everything," she looked at Grace then, her face narrowed. "He wanted to tell you everything."

She pressed the knife harder. Grace tried to back up further and felt the railing behind her give way with a light snap. She began to fall backward as Morvin backed away, and flailed out for something to grab onto.

Grace managed to grab the bottom of the terrace floor with her left hand. Her feet scrambled to get a foothold on anything but found only air. She looked up at Morvin, who smiled down at her.

"Come on, Grace," she reached out her hand. "All you have to do to save yourself is reach out with your right hand, and I'll grab it."

"Please, Morvin, help me," pleaded Grace, her grip beginning to slip. "I can't." Memories of how she received her vicious back scars returned, she could actually feel the pain of that horrid day.

"Oh, that's right...you can't. Poor, gimpy Grace, such a sad waste of space. Tsk, tsk, tsk."

"Morvin, don't do this. We're sisters. I love you."

"Sisters! We're not sisters, you revolting little idiot. I'm your mother. Your real mother." Morvin's face was ticking, her head twitching. She looked unhinged.

Grace managed to get her tiptoes on a thin ridge

below. It wasn't deep, but it gave her arm some relief from the pull of gravity. "What? What are you talking about?" she asked.

Morvin looked miles away as she revealed the ugly truth. "Wilson was getting older, so his nephew came to work here. He was nice to me. I liked him. One afternoon we snuck away to the lake at the back of the property. It was exciting, I really thought he liked me." Morvin's eyes focused in on Grace's and a mean sneer grew on her face. "He raped me that afternoon. Forced himself on me. Hurt me. I ended up pregnant...with you!"

Her lips were trembling. "You ruined my life. You ruined everything. I wanted an abortion, but they all said it was too late, that I waited too long to tell them." Tears were streaming down Morvin's face now. "I was stuck with it, while it continued to grow inside me like a vile, alien monster." Morvin had a grimace of disgust on her face as she looked down at Grace. "I should've pulled you out with a coat hanger."

"What?" Grace heard Keaton's voice from behind Morvin. Morvin whirled around. "What the hell are you talking about?" he asked her.

"Keaton! I...I...I meant to tell you," Morvin stammered.

"You lying old bitch!" Grace heard a slap, and then Keaton's face appeared over the edge. He began prying Grace's fingers off the railing. "Die, you meddling cunt!" he yelled at Grace.

He smashed Grace's fingers repeatedly with his fist, she let go and started to fall. Panic filled her body, there was nothing to grab. She was going to fall to her death.

Something flickered then in her peripheral vision,

and, for a second, time slowed. She saw the flickering of tiny wings as a white butterfly lit on a thick black electric wire that ran across the building. Grace watched as the wings on the insect beat back and forth in slow motion. She felt the thick wire brush against the back knuckles of her right hand just in front of her stomach. Even though Grace's right arm had very little strength, she somehow found the power to use it. She latched her fingers around the wire, which gave her a chance to find footing on a trellis a few feet below.

The moment passed, and time resumed its natural pace, like the play button being pushed on the remote control.

Keaton bent over the rail and watched Grace struggle with a satisfied grin. With a final crack, the rest of the railing gave way, and Keaton fell headfirst. Grace watched in horror as he landed on the garden gate below, his body impaled on the iron finials.

She heard Morvin's anguished, painful cry from above. Grace looked up and saw her looking down at her son in terror. She watched as Morvin's face turned instantly from one of extreme distress to extreme calm. Without emotion, she turned away from the edge of the terrace.

Grace carefully maneuvered her way down the trellis to the third-floor balcony. Her mind reeled as she tried to make sense of everything Morvin had said. Morvin is her mother? She killed their father? She was raised on nothing but lies. It was unbelievable.

She entered the house, thankful that the formal dining hall balcony was unlocked, and made her way to the kitchen to call the police. Just as Grace picked up the handset, she heard an ear-splitting scream from behind. She turned and saw Morvin running fast toward her, wildly slashing a knife. Morvin plunged the knife deep into Grace's abdomen.

Her strength seemed tenfold, her face twisted by insane rage. Grace managed to get hold of Morvin's wrist momentarily, but she quickly broke free. The knife came swinging down for another stab when a sudden flash of silver crashed down on Morvin's skull.

Morvin's black pupils rolled up inside her head as she fell hard to the floor. There, standing behind her, was Cameron, holding a bloody shovel. He dropped it at his side and ran to Grace.

"Oh my God, Grace. You're hurt!" he said, brushing her damp hair off her face.

Grace looked down at the blood on her shirt. The stain was spreading rapidly. "Is...is she dead?"

"I don't know," he went to Morvin's side and checked for a pulse. "No, she's alive."

Cameron grabbed a dish towel and pressed it to Grace's wound. "Hold that firmly while I call the police."

"You're bleeding too," she said when he returned to her side. "What happened?"

"Long story, just try to relax," he replied. They kept their eyes on Morvin while they waited for the police and ambulances to arrive. Morvin lay motionless. She didn't regain consciousness until the paramedics lifted her onto a gurney.

"She killed my boy! She killed my son! Arrest her! Arrest that stupid bitch!" Morvin thrashed around on the stretcher, yelling and screaming. They could still hear her as the ambulance sped away.

A second ambulance took Grace and Cameron to the hospital while the police swarmed through the house.

CHAPTER THIRTY-SIX

HER HEAVY EYES flickered open, and when they finally focused, she saw him sitting there, sleeping, still in the same spot. She smiled.

"You're still here? Have you gone home at all?" Grace asked softly. Cameron had barely left her side since she was rushed to the hospital three days ago. She thought he was the sweetest man she'd ever known.

He woke easily, probably just resting his eyes. "Aye, I went home and fed Piper, played wi' him for a bit. He says he misses you, and he bought you a present." Cameron held out another box of chocolates, the third box in so many days.

"If you keep that up, they'll have to wheel me out of here on a truck." She adjusted herself to sit up and winced. "I think I'm getting out on Friday, thank goodness. This place is so dismal."

The care in the hospital was good, but the building itself was in dire need of repair. The walls were chipped and scuffed, the floor faded and cracked. Grace cringed every time she looked around her room at the thought of all the germs that must be crawling on every surface.

"So soon? Do you think you're ready?"

"I feel better every day, just tender around the stitches." Thankfully, Morvin's knife had not damaged any internal organs and had only slightly penetrated the muscle in Grace's abdomen. "How about you? How are you feeling?"

Cameron had sustained many cuts and bruises from his ordeal in the old stable building. A few were quite deep and needed stitches but, all in all, he fared quite well.

"Ach, dinna worry about me, love. I'm fine. But I'll tell you what, you'll be staying wi' me until you're ready to—" he stopped and moved to her bedside, "Are you going back home? Back to England?"

"Wow, you look so serious," she replied, but she was glad he was concerned about her plans. "I guess I'll have to eventually. I haven't decided what to do with the house. I don't know how it's going to feel to walk back through those doors." She patted the edge of the bed, wanting him closer. "When are you going home?"

"I've still got at least another few weeks of final editing to do, so I'll be at the cottage for a while yet."

"Are the police still at Craigrook?" she asked.

So far, the investigators had discovered several vials of toxic poisons in the shed behind Morvin's garden. They had also confirmed that both Lena and Grace's mother (Grace still referred to her this way and probably always would) had died of intentional poisoning. Apparently, Morvin had been slowly poisoning her mother for weeks.

Cameron obeyed gladly and joined her, perching on the edge of the hospital bed. "Grace, police have discovered skeletal remains in the back field, behind Keaton's outbuilding. Most were the bones of animals, but some were human." She shivered at the thought of it. He continued, "They also found this in Morvin's garden shed."

He handed her an antique tin box, faded and rusty on the edges. Cameron helped her open the warped lid. Tears welled up in Grace's eyes as she took out a delicate gold chain with a beautiful pendant in the shape of a butterfly. There was also a card at the bottom of the box. She read it out loud.

"Happy fourteenth birthday, Gracey. Always remember that you are my special girl, and you can do anything you set your mind to. I have so much to tell you, so much needs to be said. Everything will be better soon, and you'll understand. For now, know that I love you, my little flutterby. Love, Dad."

Cameron put the chain around her neck, and she looked down at the pendant. Grace wrapped the fingers of her right hand around the shiny butterfly.

Cameron took her hand in his. "Would you stay with me, Grace? I mean until you're healed and you figure out what to do."

Grace couldn't imagine leaving him. She'd have fallen apart entirely if it wasn't for his support these last few days. He'd encouraged her to talk through the harsh realities she was facing. He'd helped her realize that although her past was a lie, it didn't have to damage the strong, capable woman she had become. She was falling fast for him and those caring, warm, honest blue eyes.

"Thank you, Cameron. I can't leave anyway until the will is settled, and the investigation is over. And I honestly can't imagine staying in that huge house by myself right now, especially after all that's happened. I can't stop seeing Keaton falling to his death right in front of me. The doctor says Morvin hasn't said a word since they brought her in. She saw him fall too. She must be completely devastated." Grace looked up into his handsome face. He made her feel safe, protected, and loved. "I don't know whether to sell the house or what to do with it. Do you think I should sell it?"

"I think there's no hurry, darlin'," he said with that sexy rolling 'r' of his.

"Come here," she said. She wanted to hold him close and never let go.

Cameron bent down to her, and she grabbed him by his strong shoulders and squeezed.

"Ouch," she said, feeling a pull in her stitches. "Damn. I just want to be with you, here, right now." She was a little shocked by her own directness.

"You are feeling better," he teased. "Must be all that chocolate I've been feeding you."

She smiled at him, "You really do need to stop that," she slapped him jokingly and felt another pull of the stitches. "Ow."

"Take it easy, lass, or you'll hurt yourself and end up having to stay in here longer. And I want you home wi' me." He gave her a cheeky smile that was enough to do her in. "I'll go and let you rest awhile. I'll come back tonight. Anything I can bring you, besides more sweeties?"

"Just you. Wearing nothing but a big red bow."

Cameron laughed. "Be careful what you wish for, my dear." He bent down again and softly kissed her. He smelled fantastic, as usual. She watched him leave the room and knew, without any doubt, this was it. She was his. Totally. Forever.

Grace tried to nap after Cameron left, but couldn't calm her mind. She kept thinking about Keaton's death and what that must have done to Morvin. She didn't forgive Morvin for all the things she had done, but in some way, finally understood the deep, bitter hatred she'd had for Grace all these years.

First raped and then pregnant at only twelve years old and then being forced to have the child and look at her face every day of your life, it must have been terribly painful. Obviously, it took its toll on her mental health.

Maybe going for a walk would help occupy her mind and tire her out, Grace thought. The nurses had been encouraging her to get moving anyway and had provided her with a walker for support. She tried to lean forward and pull herself up with her arm, but the pain in her abdomen was intense. She tried leaning to one side first, made it a little farther, almost upright, but again had to back off from the burning, pulling agony. She begrudgingly pushed the call button, and a few minutes later, a perky, smiling young nurse came to help.

Grace shuffled to the elevator and took it to the main floor. She browsed a small gift shop and giggled at a collection of newborn onesies with cute sayings. One she liked, in particular, had a *Star Wars* logo and read, 'Stormpooper.'

She began feeling quite sore and decided to rest by a window. A young girl and her mum were seated across from her. The girl was eating ice cream, and her IV tube kept pulling painfully every time she scooped another spoonful. The mother didn't notice, she was too busy on her phone. Grace got up and headed back to the elevator. As she passed the child, she unhooked her stuck IV tube from the top of the pole so that it no longer pulled. The girl looked warily at Grace but gave her a slight smile, her mother still oblivious. Grace smiled back.

In the elevator, Grace glanced at a map of the hospital. She saw that the psychiatric ward was located on the second floor, one floor down from hers. As the doors were closing, Grace shook her head and hastily pushed number two.

Grace pushed her walker up to the desk and said, "Is it possible to see Morvin Knowles?"

A large nurse with a thick neck replied, "Who wants to see her? It's family only, at the moment." The nurse raised her eyebrows at Grace in question. She was wearing Snoopy scrubs.

"I'm her sister...er," Grace stammered, "yes, her sister."

"Sign in here," she said and handed Grace a form attached to a clipboard.

As Grace signed the form, she asked the austere nurse, "How has she been?"

"Never a problem. In fact, Ms. Knowles hasn't said a word since she got here. We're keeping her calm with sedation but keep things nice and mellow when you see her, all right?"

"Of course," said Grace.

She led Grace to an antiseptic, impersonal television lounge that a few other patients were occupying. The walls were painted putty-pink, adding to the room's cold, unwelcome atmosphere. A bake-off program aired unwatched in a far corner on an old television. The host's plastic voice echoed off the blank walls.

One woman, maybe in her twenties, sat in a wheelchair, off by herself in front of a barred window. She was pulling out thick clumps of her hair, seemingly oblivious to the pain it must have caused. She would then open her hand, let it go, and watch it fall to the ground. Another woman sat in a wooden rocking chair, weeping non-stop. Someone else down the hall screamed at the top of their lungs like they were being tortured.

How can anyone get well in this place? Grace wondered.

They wheeled Morvin into the room, and her appearance astounded Grace. She must have aged twenty years in the past week. She held her head in her hands, not once looking up at Grace.

"Morvin? Hi, Morvin, how are you feeling?" Grace asked in a low voice. No response. She tried again.

"Morvin? It's me, Grace."

Then everything went haywire. In an instant, Grace found herself gasping for air, staring into Morvin's wild, bloodshot eyes. Spit flew through her clenched teeth as she tried with all her strength to squeeze the life out of Grace.

She kept growling, "Die, you bitch, die, you bitch."

It took three nurses and one orderly to get Morvin off of her. As they carried her away she just kept yelling, "*DIE, DIE, DIE!*"

Grace's neck was scratched, bleeding, and badly

bruised. Tears streamed down her cheeks as a nurse saw to her fresh wounds. She couldn't wait to get out of there but was asked to stay and file a report on Morvin. When she was finished, an orderly pushed her back up to her room in a wheelchair. She was glad for that, her legs felt like rubber. Grace knew now she had to face the fact that there was simply no hope for Morvin. Maybe there never was.

CHAPTER THIRTY-SEVEN

GRACE WAS PUTTING her belongings into the bag Cameron had brought her the night before. She was finally being discharged this morning.

She'd barely slept a wink last night, tossing and turning for hours. She sat up to puff her flat, pathetic excuse for a pillow when she felt she was being watched. Grace looked nervously at the chair at the end of her bed and saw Morvin sitting there quietly, looking at her.

Grace called out to her, "Morvin? What are you doing here?"

Morvin didn't answer, just sat there, her head bent at an odd angle and her eyes bulging grossly out of her head. There was no noise from the ward beyond the door. Where was the constant beeping, the ever-present hum of activity from outside the door? Dead silence hung in the air between them.

"Morvin, what do you want?" Grace swallowed hard, her mouth dry as cotton. She pulled the thin hospital blanket up to her neck.

Morvin began to groan softly, as she reached out a skinny gray hand toward Grace. She reached out both arms, her bony fingers like claws ready to rip the flesh from Grace's face.

Grace backed up in the bed, trying to put as much distance between them as possible. Then Morvin came at her fast, a loud shriek escaping her mouth through jagged, bloody teeth. Grace shielded her face with her arm and screamed. Then...nothing. It was like Morvin had passed right through her.

The sounds from the ward slowly returned as Grace's breath slowed to normal. She was freezing yet clammy with sweat. Was that a dream? Did she scream out loud? When no nurse came running, she assumed not. It must have been a nightmare.

She looked at the time on her phone: 5:23 a.m. She got out of bed and splashed water on her face. Grace paced anxiously and waited until seven o'clock, when she could call Cameron to pick her up early. She couldn't wait to get out of that room and back to Cameron's, where she could convalesce by the fire in his warm, inviting cottage. The sooner she put this cold, grim room behind her, the better.

Grace took another look around, taking care that she wasn't leaving anything behind. They'd need to make a few trips to get all the flowers and chocolates down to the car. Not to mention the enormous teddy bear Cameron had brought her last night. As he struggled to get it through the door, you couldn't even see him behind it; just a giant stuffed bear pushing its way into her room.

The doctor had kept Grace in an extra couple of days, and she was becoming depressed because of it. She felt fine, why the torture? Cameron had been trying to perk her up by sneaking in some of his spaghetti and a small bottle of red wine that he hid in the teddy bear's pants. They sipped the wine from small paper cups, it went right to Grace's head.

The two felt like a couple of teenagers having almost been caught getting carried away in her tiny hospital bed. Thankfully, the nurse had walked in backward while talking to someone, giving them time to fix themselves.

Grace wore a coquettish grin as she zipped up her bag, playing the moment back in her mind. Thoughts of him made her feel all wiggly inside, she was absolutely giddy with love for him.

She heard the familiar whoosh of the door opening and felt her heart skip as he walked in.

"Hello there, my beauty. Ready to come home?" He brushed up against her back and kissed the side of her neck.

She tingled inside and turned to him, kissed him firmly, and whispered, "Oh yes."

Cameron loaded up the car and brought up a wheelchair.

"No, you can't be serious. I can walk fine for heaven's sake."

"I know, but apparently it's hospital policy," said Cameron.

"Well, I'll take it to the elevator, but after that, forget it."

A middle-aged nurse approached them as they passed

the nurses' station. "Miss Calhoun, the doctor is discharging you on the condition that you'll have help at home, dear," She looked like she had just worked a twenty-hour shift; sweaty hair, tired eyes. "Is this the case?" She gave Cameron a full head to toe scan, over her reading glasses.

"Yes, I'll be in good hands," said Grace as she stood up out of the wheelchair.

Cameron winked and nodded his head enthusiastically, as the nurse looked back at her clipboard.

"And there are to be no strenuous activities for at least another couple of days," she continued.

"Well, I'm afraid we canny guarantee that one," Cameron said with a laugh. Grace swatted him in the arm.

"Mmm, hmm," the tired nurse gave Cameron a dirty look, "Sign here, please."

Grace signed the form and took a seat in the wheelchair. Cameron was still chuckling as he wheeled her to the elevator. He pushed the call button with his elbow. "Germs," he said. But it came out as 'jehrrrams' with his accent.

"Excuse me, Miss Calhoun?"

Grace and Cameron turned around.

A doctor was approaching them. "I just need a word in private, miss." His expression was dour.

Foreboding filled her as she looked up at Cameron. "Okay," she said. "But anything you say can be said in front of my...uh, my friend."

The doctor motioned for them to follow and led them to a quiet seating area at the end of the long hall. "I'm afraid I've got some terrible news for you," he said. He seemed dressed beyond his years in brown slacks and a drab tie. The fact that he was balding only added to his aging appearance, but his skin was smooth and unwrinkled. He was either old looking for his age or aging really well. It was hard to tell.

"Okay. What is it?" Grace steeled herself.

"It concerns Morvin Knowles. She is your sister, correct?"

"Yes, well...yes, she's my sister." Grace decided not to get into particulars at present.

"I'm afraid she was found dead early this morning. It seems she used her own hospital gown to hang herself. A nurse discovered her early this morning, but she had been there for at least a couple of hours. It was too late for any hope of saving her, I'm afraid."

Grace was speechless.

"Okay, thank you, doctor," said Cameron. "Is there someone we need to call?"

The doctor scratched a number on a card and handed it to Cameron. "So sorry about the news. Take care of yourselves."

"C'mon, hen, let's get you home."

They drove without a word for quite a while. Cameron wanted to talk about it but wasn't sure how to start. Then Grace broke the silence.

"I guess this means it's actually all mine then. The money," Grace looked at Cameron. "It's so weird. I didn't want any of it. My whole life, I vowed never to ask for a dime, now the whole damn thing is in my lap. It's surreal, you know?" She turned her head and looked out her window.

"It is definitely one for the books," he said. "I'll give you that. Are you okay, about the news...about Morvin?"

"Strangely, Cameron, I am," she kept her gaze on the fleeting scenery. "I have to be."

CHAPTER THIRTY-EIGHT

"HELLO, CROSSFIELD MORGUE, I mean Books."

"Hi, Wesley," Grace said into her new cell phone.

"Whoops, sorry 'bout that, boss-lady, been a little slow today," he said.

"Glad we're up and running again, though," she said.

"That's for sure. How's it going, Grace? Have you heard anything from my brother yet?" Wesley stopped what he was doing and took a seat at the register.

"No, you guys haven't heard from him either? That's strange. I hope he's okay."

"Wouldn't be the first time he's gone missing in action without a word. I wouldn't worry too much yet, Grace. He probably came across a traveling bikini convention and we won't hear from him for months." He chuckled. "When are you coming home?"

"I'm actually on my way now. I should be there in a few hours." Grace was looking so forward to seeing her friends and, of course, her cat Ernie.

"Awesome. I'll let Devi know. She's coming round the shop with samosas in a bit," Wesley said.

"That's perfect. Oh my gosh, I've missed Devita's cooking. I can't wait to see you guys." Grace looked out her window at the scenery flying by. The country was so beautiful, but she loved the city as well, and she loved her business and especially her best friends.

Grace had made some huge decisions and hoped they were the right ones. In the end, she went with her heart and made her choice final. Life is about choices when you come across forks in the road. At some point we all have to take risks. It's not living if we don't.

"Yeah, we've kind of missed you too," Wesley said sarcastically. He crooked the phone in his ear while he took a sip of his Pepsi.

"How's Ernest?" she asked.

"He's good. Misses you, though. He gets this look of disappointment when I walk through the door. The nasty cat's starting to hurt my feelings."

Grace could hear him slurping the last of his fizzy drink. "Still chugging down the liquid sugar, I hear."

"Oh yeah, sorry," he put the pop down. "What time will you be here?"

Grace looked at the clock on her dash. "Should be there about six-thirty, if the traffic cooperates."

"Sounds good. Umm, Grace?" he said, suddenly a bit quieter.

"Yes?"

"I'm happy you're coming home," he cleared his throat.

She imagined his face getting flushed, and she smiled. She'd missed him so much, missed her home. "Me too, Wes," she replied. "See you soon."

She turned the speaker on her cell phone off and almost missed the entrance to the freeway. She veered the car quickly to the right, swearing at herself under her breath, and drove over the dirt shoulder just in time. As she righted herself and began to gain speed to merge with the freeway traffic, she failed to notice the black SUV following her a few car lengths behind.

She used her key and entered the bookstore from the back. Grace could smell smoke slightly, but Devi was right, the damage was minimal.

She could hear Wesley and Devi chatting upfront, Wesley talking through a mouthful of samosas. Grace never thought she'd miss their bantering as much as she did. It was great to hear their voices again. She felt like she'd been gone for months instead of a few weeks.

Grace snuck quietly up to the front of the shop, keeping close to the walls. Once she was close enough to hopefully scare the pants off them, she yelled, "Hi!"

Both their heads swung round in surprise and shock.

"You bugger," said Devi.

"Holy shit!" exclaimed Wesley.

"I'm sorry, guys. I couldn't resist." Grace laughed as she hurried over to hug them.

Devi squeezed her back, hard. "I called you a couple of times, Gracey. I left messages. Why didn't you get back? I was worried." Her eyebrows were pulled down, furrowed, an expression she often wore, even though she was the kindest woman on the planet. Grace had seen Devi's mother with the same sour face many times.

"I know Devi, I'm sorry. I lost my cell phone, and I was dealing with so much. It was a nightmare. I'll explain everything later, I promise. But first, I want to welcome you to...my new bookstore!" Grace swept her arms through the air like a game show model.

"What?" the two friends said in unison.

"Yeah. I bought the place from Armin. Offered him a price he couldn't resist. We'll be able to fix it up, Wes." He was gobsmacked, staring at her, not saying anything. "We can get the fireplace working again and put in those wingbacks you talked about."

"How?" asked Devi. "How can you afford this?"

"Yeah," added Wes.

"As I said, I'll go into full detail later. Suffice it to say, money isn't an issue for me right now, and, if I'm smart about it, it won't ever be." Grace handed a set of new keys to Wesley. "These are yours, Wesley, if you'll have them."

"What do you mean?"

"I need you to run the place, as the manager, I mean. With a manager's wage, of course." She looked at Devi, "I've decided to stay in Scotland, live there, and restore my family estate. And also...I've met someone."

"Okay," said Devi, crossing her arms, a cheeky grin on her face. "Let's have it."

"All in due time, girlfriend," she looked back at Wesley. "So, what do you say? I'll come back often and check on things, do the books, that sort of thing, but you'll be in full charge." She raised her eyebrows at him, awaiting his answer.

He looked dazed as he glanced around the treasured little store. Then he turned to Grace and, with a huge grin, said, "How about freakin' *yes!*"

"Yay!" Grace was bouncing up and down, her hands interlaced under her chin. She hugged him again. "Come outside. I've got something else to show you."

They followed her out to the sidewalk in front of the store. Grace grabbed a rope that was attached to a cover over the hanging store sign. She made a drumroll noise as she pulled the cord, revealing newly installed signage.

"The Dusty Shelf!" said Wesley. "I can't believe it! It's so awesome. Wait, when did you do this?"

"Glad you like it. It's a great name. I'm so glad I thought of it," Grace teased.

"Hey!" he punched Grace in the arm. "Cheeky woman. Aren't you going to miss the place though, Grace? I mean, you love this store."

"I do, Wesley, you're right, but after I get the estate fixed up, I'm hoping to open another, in Scotland, if I can find the right building and, of course, if we can make this one work.

"Another Dusty Shelf. Hey, there's your name for it," Wesley said, beaming. "You're welcome."

Grace laughed as she grabbed her purse and locked

the door. "Let's go eat. I'm starved. I know this great little Indian joint around the corner." She winked at Devi and put her arms around them both as they walked down the sidewalk to Devi's café.

CHAPTER THIRTY-NINE

GRACE EASED HERSELF into the hot, steaming water. She inhaled deeply and then exhaled long and slow, letting go of any and all tension in her body.

A few days ago, she had received a call from the police, asking her to come in and identify a male body found on the shore of Blackmore River. She couldn't be one hundred percent positive that it was Marc because his face was disfigured and severely bloated from the water. She did recognize his jet black hair and one gold-cross earring. Dental records, however, had confirmed that it was Marc Foster. The cause of death was apparently a massive blow to the head.

Would this nightmare ever end?

Apparently, Marc had been at a neighborhood pub well into the evening. He'd had a lot to drink and decided to walk back to his hotel when he was struck by a speeding car. Some young man confessed his and Keaton's involvement after his mother noticed blood on the hood of her car.

Poor Wesley. Grace felt responsible, because Marc had only come to Scotland to see if she was all right. She hired Marc's architectural firm to do the restoration on Craigrook, a kind of homage to honor his memory.

Grace sank into the hot water, trying to ease her sore muscles. The contractors wanted to begin insulating as soon as next week, so Grace had tackled packing the large storage room on the top floor. There was so much junk in there: LP records, film reels, old clothing, even eight-track tapes. Why did her mother hang on to that stuff?

In one corner, there was a white sheet draped over something wide and low to the ground. Grace hesitated to uncover it. These walls held so much pain and betrayal that it felt like an actual presence existed. Grace hoped, with renovations, and a good purge and cleaning, that ominous feeling would fade.

She finally pulled the sheet off, releasing years of dust in the process. Grace coughed and waved it away, then smiled with surprise at her old dollhouse. She bent down in front of it and opened the front swinging façade, remembering how she played with it for hours on end. It was still in great shape.

The mommy doll, Grace could tell by the blue apron with lace trim it wore, was lying on the floor of the small kitchen. When she picked it up, the head fell off. *Sad,* thought Grace, *how did that happen?* She picked up the daddy doll that was lying in the miniature study and found the same thing, his head was broken as well.

One of the girl dolls was in the first-floor sitting room, seated in a floral armchair. This one was fully intact. Grace searched through the little replica house for her favorite doll, the one she always thought of as herself. There it was, in the bedroom that matched her own. It looked intact as well on the first inspection, but Grace dropped it promptly after picking it up. Sharp pieces of wood and wire were stabbed all over the little body, and it was drawn all over with red ink. Even the face was 'bleeding.'

Wow, Morvin really was one sick woman. Revolted, Grace covered the dollhouse again, saddened by the thought that she'd have to get rid of it now. She couldn't pass it down one day to her own children with that type of malevolence having occurred within its little walls.

Grace shivered in the claw foot tub as she replayed the image of the doll over in her mind. "Let it go," she said quietly and closed her eyes. She sank deeper into the water and let it envelop her entirely, savoring the warmth in her bones. The old house never seemed to get warm enough. That would improve, though, with the restoration plans started, which included updates to the central heating and insulation.

She couldn't wait to show the initial plans for Craigrook to Cameron. He was in Glasgow for a couple of days, meeting with his agent and taking care of a few things at home. He was supposed to be back at Craigrook tomorrow morning, and Grace couldn't wait. She'd never had let him leave her in the house alone if it wasn't for Piper, her faithful bodyguard.

Grace and Cameron had been practically inseparable since she returned from England, and she missed him desperately.

She lay there and listened to the natural noises in the

room, in the house. A relic like this was always making settling noises, like old bones shifting and creaking after another long day's work. She could also hear the rain and wind outside, made louder by the raindrops pelting off the first-floor roof that was just below the bathroom window. All the noises amplified in the spacious, clinically white bathroom.

Grace wrung out a facecloth and placed it on her forehead. The faucet was steadily plinking droplets of water into the bath.

She opened her eyes as she heard another sound, a different one. *Maybe it's the wind,* thought Grace. *Yeah, it's just the wind.* The way it swirled around the many edges and corners of the building made it whistle and howl in different pitches and decibels.

There it was again. Grace sat up in the bath as she tried to identify the noise; it sounded like the creaky stairway. Her fear heightened as Piper started barking.

She rushed out of the bath and wrapped herself in her dressing gown. Piper let out a loud, distressing yelp. She called out for the dog and was just about to turn the glass doorknob when the door burst open in her face! It was him. The man from the night at the library. He was holding the same large knife that he threatened to skin her with, and he looked angry enough to make good on his promise to use it.

Grace backed away from him, looking for anything she could use as a weapon. There was nothing.

"Just because the little weasel is dead doesn't mean his debts are forgotten. You're going to pay up tonight, or your bathing days are over." He loomed over Grace. He was absolutely enormous.

She ducked down beside him, under his arm, and ran to the other side of the room, nearly slipping on the wet tile floor. She stood facing him from the opposite side of the bathtub.

"Okay. That's no problem. How much is it? I can get it from the bank and have it for you by tomorrow." Grace said, tremor in her voice. He was definitely well over six feet tall and at least two-hundred and fifty pounds. He had thinning, black hair that was wet and stuck to his scalp in thin strands; some stray hairs were plastered to his nasty, scarred face.

He reached across the tub and almost had Grace by her wrap, but she forcefully tore free. There was nowhere to run. He was too big, and his arms had a wide span, he grabbed her as she tried to run past.

He wrapped a massive arm around her neck and squeezed tightly. Grace bent her head and bit deep into his wrist while at the same time jabbing her heel hard into his foot. Then, remembering her kickboxing classes, she spun around and brought her right foot up, kicking him as hard as she could in the scrotum. He bent over in pain, and Grace took the opportunity to run, but he grabbed her by the ankle, and she slammed, face first, onto the solid, unforgiving tiles.

Grace was dazed as she felt herself being carried out of the bathroom. He took her to one of the bedrooms and laid her on the large bed. Though she was dazed from her fall, she recognized this was her mother's room.

He was breathing heavily, his breath sour, like too many late-afternoon pints.

"Now, let's have a look-see at what's under this robe, you lively little bitch." His voice was deep and gravelly.

He straddled her body and held her arms out at her side, his eyes explored her body where her gown had fallen open. She struggled under his strong hold. Once more, she brought up her leg and, with her knee this time, jammed him in the crotch. Without much leverage, she couldn't get a ton of force behind it, but he must have still been tender from the first blow. He released her left arm just enough that she got it free and grabbed the first thing she could get her hand on. She hit him on the temple with the old, metal music box from the nightstand. He grabbed his head in agony and rolled onto his side.

Grace made a run for the door. He was coming, but he was moving a little slower. It was now or never. She had to stop him, or he'd soon get his strength back and come after her again. He staggered toward her, still bent over. One hand on his crotch and the other, the knife-wielding hand, on his bleeding face. She brought the music box down again, steel feet first, onto the middle of his skull. He faltered on his feet and began to fall backward. His head hit the corner of the large wooden dressing table with a thick, sickening smack. His large frame thumped to the floor, and he fell on his side.

Still holding her makeshift weapon, Grace walked to where he lay, ready to hit him again if he moved. There was blood pooling fast under his shoulder, and she saw that the blade of his own knife was stuck in his neck.

"Oh my God, Piper," Grace said and left the room at a run. "Piper! Piper!" She heard whining coming from the foyer closet, and she swung open the door. "Are you okay, buddy?"

She gave him a quick once over, checking for blood and wounds. It was hard to examine him, though, he was wiggling all over and planting big kisses on her face. "Okay, okay, you're all right."

She went to the kitchen and called 911 for the second time in just a few short months.

CHAPTER FORTY

G RACE FELT A flutter in her stomach at the thought of Cameron coming home. He should be walking in the door any minute now.

She had called him after what happened with the maniac, whose name, she learned from investigators, was Bruce Michaels. Apparently, he was a 'leg breaker' for some shady casino owner in Edinburgh; someone Keaton owed over ten thousand pounds. Police had been trying to find something concrete to pin on the crooked lender for months. Attempted murder was precisely what they needed.

Cameron wanted to come home immediately after she told the whole story, but Grace assured him she was fine. The madman was dead; the nightmare was over.

Thank goodness Piper was okay. Michaels had grabbed

the dog and thrown him in a closet that night, but Piper suffered no severe injuries. It was his barking that confirmed someone was in the house, and she'd be eternally grateful to him for that. Grace looked down at the dog as he snoozed by her feet under the desk. She scratched his head, and Piper groaned with approval.

Finalizing the restoration and renovation plans for Craigrook kept Grace busy. Marc's firm had been doing outstanding work; she loved the ideas they had for her home. It would still have all the historic bones intact but with modern, updated elegance.

Landscaping construction was underway, and yesterday Grace had watched with a sense of closure as an excavator took its first bite out of Morvin's noxious frog pond. Her horrific ordeal was in the past, and she was excited to get on with her new life.

She'd always wonder, of course, what happened to her father, how he really died, but that truth was buried with Morvin. Grace touched her butterfly pendant. At least she knew he loved her and had wanted to tell her the truth. She was thankful she knew that much.

The knowledge that Morvin was her mother had rocked Grace to her center. She wasn't sure if she'd ever make peace with that. It did help, however, to understand Morvin's cruelty all those years and also helped Grace accept that it was never her fault.

She still wrestled with her decision to keep the money that she always vowed never to depend on. But Grace took solace in the fact that she was restoring her family's historic estate with it. She had also donated to a teen pregnancy charity and a portion of it to psychiatric research.

Grace heard a car pull up outside.

"Cameron!" She bumped her knee on the desk and splashed coffee on her papers. "Ouch. Easy, Grace."

She rushed to the front door and threw it open. She ran toward Cameron's smiling face, and he picked her up in his arms. He swung her around and kissed her.

"My God, I've missed you, lassie."

Piper swirled around the two of them, waiting for his turn to greet his master.

"I'm so glad you're home, Cameron." Her eyes began to water. She had no idea she could love someone this much. "Come on, I've got something to show you," she said.

"Oh, that sounds promising, but can I at least unpack first?" Cameron winked and then bent down and greeted his faithful dog, letting him soak his face with kisses.

"Stop it," she said and gave him a swat in the arm. "Seriously, get your cute little buns in here."

He looked behind him as if trying to see his 'little' buns, and she grabbed his arm, pulling him into the library.

"Look. The plans are finalized. I just need your official stamp of approval for the interior." She looked back and forth from the plans to his face, clasping her hands in front of her.

"Okay, let's see. Looks good here," Cameron said, scanning. "What's this? Is this the library? Where we're standing?"

"Yes." She tilted her head at him slightly. "Looks quite different, doesn't it? That's because it's going to be your office and personal library."

"It looks spectacular. Thank you," Cameron said, and kissed the top of Grace's head.

He continued perusing the papers, nodding here and

there. "The kitchen's going to be great. I see you went with my idea of adding the butcher block island here."

"Yes, the contractor totally loved that."

"Bloody great work, darling," he put the plans back on the desk.

"You're not done looking yet, Mister," Grace teased.

Cameron looked at the plans again. "Well, I see the master bedroom, the new en suite bathroom...lovely..." he trailed off. His face sobered. "What's this wee room here going to be used for?"

"That's the nursery, Cameron." She bit her bottom lip, waiting for him to say something.

His eyes suddenly widened, he put his hand to his mouth. "Are you saying...? I'm going to be a father?"

"Yes."

He scooped her into his arms and held her. "I can't believe it, Grace. Are you sure?"

She nodded, and a tear ran down her cheek.

"Thank you, Grace. Oh my God, a baby." He let go and looked at her through his own tears. "I guess I was a little late then."

"Late for what? What are you talking about?" she asked.

He reached into his pocket and pulled out a little blue velvet box with a shiny gold ribbon tied around its center.

Without even opening it, she screamed excitedly, "Yes! Yes! Yes!"

"You better open it before you say anything. Maybe it's just a brooch," he chided.

"It better not be." She unwrapped the ribbon and opened the little box. It practically lit up the room with its sparkle. The diamond was enormous, round in shape and set on a floral crown of, what looked like, a million dazzling diamond accents. It was absolutely exquisite.

He took the box from her, lifted out the ring, and went down on one knee. He motioned for her hand and then placed the ring gently on her finger.

Grace felt light-headed as she nodded and said, once again, "Yes."

They embraced for an eternity, both of them in tears and beyond bliss. She was so thrilled she almost forgot her other surprise. She held out a small stack of typewritten pages in front of him.

"What's this? You didn't. Already?"

"Yeah, I did. Well, it's only the outline, but it's a good start. I came up with a title for my book, too," she said, pointing to the top of the first page.

"*Finding Grace,*" he read. He smiled at her and put his arm around her shoulders. "Exactly."

Grace didn't notice the pretty white butterfly outside the library window. It sailed off in an instant and resumed its long, happy, graceful journey home.

9 781777 214913